LITTLE LEAGUE STEPSON

By Curtis Bishop

Little League Victory

Fast Break

Gridiron Glory

Little League Visitor

Sideline Pass

Little League Stepson

Little League Amigo

Lonesome End

Rebound

Little League Double Play

Sideline Quarterback

Little League Heroes

Lank of the Little League

Field Goal

Little League
Stepson

⊗ CURTIS BISHOP

J. B. Lippincott Company

PHILADELPHIA

NEW YORK

To Walter Benson

Contents

CHAPTER 1

A New Father—Just Like That!

Robin Scott had seen the tall man before, more times than he could count, in fact. But never like this—as his stepfather!

Tears flooded his eyes; he could not hold them back.

"Are you so surprised, dear?"

The question came from his mother, of course.

Robin bobbed his head.

"I have been giving you hints all along." His mother was trying to smile, but not succeeding very well. "You have seen a great deal of Chase. I was sure you knew— everything but the date."

Robin nodded. Mr. Alloway had been a regular visitor, all right. And his mother had received no other male visitors in several weeks.

"We meant to tell you ahead of time," explained his mother, "but we decided just to go over to the justice of the peace and—well, we saw no reason not to go today. I decided against a formal engagement, with an announcement in the newspaper or a church wedding. Why should there be any ceremony about a widow's second marriage?"

Robin had no answer. He understood why his mother wanted no fuss or big gathering. He had been required to attend a cousin's wedding and it had bored him from start to finish. Everybody had cried, including the cousin, and then some of his cousin's friends had acted silly afterward, laughing and snickering as if it were a big joke. Robin had seen nothing either to laugh about or cry over.

But this was different. This was his mother. The words of Aunt Martha came back to him. "Just you wait," she had said between sobs. "Your mother will marry again one of these days, and then you will cry yourself."

And he did feel a little like it. His mother said that Chase Alloway was his new father. And that was not true. A boy had only one father, and Roger Scott was buried in Oakwood Cemetery. He had died in a collision with a speeding truck and Robin had been seriously injured in the same accident. The Scott family car had burst into flames and Robin had suffered severe burns about his neck and shoulders.

"We are not going away on a honeymoon," the new Mrs. Alloway said. "Chase will move into our home. Do you want to help him bring his things over?"

Robin frowned. He had promised to help Dave Presley

and Mark Kelly work on their racer. Mark had finished second in the local soapbox derby the year before and was full of ideas for rebuilding his vehicle.

"I sort of promised Mark . . ."

"Then go play with Mark," Mr. Alloway said quickly. "I haven't very much to move anyhow. I was one bachelor without a hobby, except Little League baseball." He squeezed Robin's shoulder. "We have that interest in common anyhow, son."

"Yes, sir," Robin said.

"Don't be late," his mother said as he started for the door. "We'll have smothered steak and onions for dinner. I want my new husband to realize he has married a good cook."

"Yes, ma'am," Robin promised.

But he had lost all desire to work on the racer by the time he reached the corner of Bonnie Road and Exposition Boulevard. He sat down on the curb and flipped last year's acorns at imaginary targets. He should not be so upset; there had been every indication that his attractive mother had already decided to marry again, with Mr. Alloway as her certain choice. Mrs. Edwards, who lived just across the street, had warned Robin only the previous morning: "You are going to have a new father one of these fine days. And there is no better catch around than Chase Alloway. Good looking, successful in his profession—a fine man any way you look at him."

Robin took a deep breath. He should not be unhappy at all. If the choice had been his, he would have selected

Mr. Alloway over all the men who had vied for his mother's favor. He had known Mr. Alloway even before the tall man's first appearance at the Scott residence.

How could Robin help knowing—by sight, at least—the four managers of the West Austin Little League? They did the selecting for the major league teams; every boy wishing to play baseball tried out before these coaches. Robin had done so twice. Both times he had been passed over in the auction and assigned to a minor league club, as were all unsuccessful candidates. Robin supposed that the same thing would happen this year, even if he was eleven now, one of the "older" boys.

Yes, he had known Chase Alloway for two years, but no better than he knew Jim Tracy of the Giants, Sneaker Kane of the Cats and Mac Collins of the Dodgers. All had been aloof and forbidding figures to him, men who studied a small host of eager boys and somehow chose their new players. How they decided or when nobody knew for sure, at least no one who could explain the process to Robin Scott. He had heard some adults complain that either politics or an eenie-meenie-mienie-moe method decided which boys would get the coveted full uniforms and the privilege of playing on Knebel Field, leaving simple T-shirts for all others. Nobody, said these men and women, could test boys fairly in so short a tryout period.

Robin had not minded his failure as a nine-year-old; not many boys so young were selected. But last year—

the memory of that experience still hurt when he thought of it, and Mr. Alloway had figured in the unhappy experience, the same man who was supposedly going to take his father's place.

Robin had hit solidly in the tryouts last year, and had been one of the some thirty boys called back for further tests.

He recalled that quite clearly. The league president had read off the names of candidates the managers wanted to appraise again.

Mark Kelly and Dave Presley had been on the list, but not Robin—not until Chase Alloway had spoken up.

"Could we have No. 27 back too? Scott, isn't it—Robin Scott?"

The president had agreed and Robin had returned a second day. Midway through that drill the list had been trimmed to sixteen and Robin had been one of those left to hang around and watch or go home—the managers did not care.

Robin had gone home and to his upstairs room to cry a while because he had known why he was dismissed and why he would fail every time. He had decided that day to reject assignment to a minor league club, but his mother had talked him into changing his mind.

"You need the physical activity," she had reasoned. "You need it more than the other boys. Besides, you enjoy playing."

And so he had played. And he had posted a high batting average and acquitted himself fairly well at first base, the only position Mr. Carowe said he could play——

"Hi, Scott!"

Mark Kelly called to him from a block away, coming on as fast as he could pump his bicycle.

"I thought you were working on your racer?"

"I thought you were going to help."

"I was. But——" Robin hesitated. "Something happened over at my house."

"My mother just told me." Mark sat down by Robin. "That's why I hustled over here. I'll bet you sure are tickled."

"Not much."

"You ought to be, that's for sure. Chase Alloway is a smart manager."

Robin flipped another acorn. "His team never has won a championship. Besides, that won't help me."

"Everybody says he is a good manager. My dad said that if he had had the pitching last year—I'll sure play for him, if he'll take me."

Neither Mark nor Dave had won major league berths either.

"He will help you," Mark went on. "He can even take you on the team, if he wants to. Even assistant managers can take their own boys. They don't even have to bid. That's how Bruce Elliott made a team when he was eight years old. Mr. Alloway's team, too."

Robin shook his head. He had never been jealous of the sixty proud boys in the major circuit.

"Bruce could make any team in the league." Robin

stood up suddenly. He was in no humor to talk with anyone, even Mark. "Mom said to be home for early supper," he explained rather lamely.

Yet he did not want to go home either. He must get over this feeling, he brooded. Yet how could he, just like that? It was one thing to think of Mr. Alloway as a man who took his mother places and sent her flowers; a succession of men had been doing that for the last two years. But as for taking his father's place, that was entirely different. Mr. Alloway was sitting in the chair Robin's father had called his own, reading the afternoon paper which Robin usually opened and read first.

"How is Mark?" Mr. Alloway asked pleasantly as Robin came in.

"Fine."

"Is he coming out for the league again?"

"Sure. He'll be a cinch to make it this year——" Robin hesitated, remembering too late that he was talking to one of the managers. "He sure did well in the minor league last season."

"So did you," said Mr. Alloway.

Robin's mother came in from the kitchen. She was wearing a brief apron over her jersey dress.

"Robin was in the starting lineup every game," she said proudly. "And he was a dependable hitter. Mr. Carowe said so."

Robin ducked his head. His mother should not say such things.

Mr. Alloway smiled at his new wife. "I know about Robin," he said lightly. "He made a fairly good showing in the tryouts last year. I had him called back for a second trial."

"*You* did?"

"Yes." His eyes twinkled. "I knew your son, Mrs. Alloway, before I was introduced to you. Robin showed a good eye at the plate, but held his elbows too high. That fault can be corrected, of course. But he was slow afoot and——"

Robin's mother started to explain that shortcoming; the boy shook his head at her. She stopped herself in time.

"But this is another season," Mr. Alloway added. "I know ways to work a boy into shape. I should; I've been doing it a long time."

His wife sat down. "I am glad you and Robin have baseball in common; it will help you get to know each other sooner. You *will* help him, won't you?"

"Sure. Shall we start tomorrow afternoon, Robin?"

"You mean start practicing?"

"Sure."

Robin hesitated. He had not thought much about baseball yet. Then he saw the appeal in his mother's eyes.

"Yes, sir. I'm on safety patrol, but——"

"You get home by four-thirty," his mother pointed out.

"That's as soon as I can get through," Mr. Alloway said. "Where is your glove?"

"In your top drawer," Robin's mother said as he hesitated. "And your bat is under your bed."

Robin produced both. His stepfather carefully examined the leather object which had served Robin for two seasons.

"Your mother picked it out, didn't she?"

Mrs. Alloway answered for herself. "Of course. What is wrong with it?"

"Just not enough of a glove," the manager said casually. A smile touched his lean features. "I'll bet you started off with a first baseman's mitt, too."

Again Mrs. Alloway answered. "Was that wrong?"

"Exactly wrong," Mr. Alloway said calmly. "So is this glove. I believe in a three-fingered model for boys just starting out. I'll take Robin to a sporting goods store tomorrow——"

"Robin is *not* just starting out. He has already played two years."

"He is just starting, and he realizes it," Mr. Alloway said. "Don't you, Robin?"

The boy's answering nod came slowly. The other boys said there was all the difference in the world between the minor league game and the major league version.

Mr. Alloway studied the bat next. "Too heavy," was his grunted verdict. "We'll get a bat, too. I'll pick you up at school, Robin."

Again an eloquent look from his mother silenced Robin. He rode home on his bicycle on clear days and enjoyed it. But for a new glove and bat——

He should feel happier than he did, he told himself before dropping off to sleep that night. Since he *must* have a stepfather, it was great that his mother had chosen a Little League manager. But how different was Chase Alloway from his father! Roger Scott was a quiet sort of man who had preferred hunting and fishing to spectator sports. And his mother—how had she become interested in Mr. Alloway? She liked to read; she wrote book reviews for the local newspaper. She preferred classical music to the popular style; she had threatened him with bodily damage if he grew into a "bop" lover. Chase Alloway was a former professional football player. He still officiated in high school games in addition to managing his Little League team. It did not make sense, but married they were.

And Mr. Alloway even talked as if he could develop Robin into a Little League player. That would not happen, of course. Mr Alloway did not not know exactly what he was up against.

CHAPTER 2

Robin's First Lesson

MR. ALLOWAY had several baseballs left over from the previous season; the bat and glove purchased, they were ready for practice. Robin expected to be taken to the West Austin field, but his stepfather said the back yard would do.

"Ever play pepper?"

Robin shook his head.

"You can practice all the fundamentals in a small space," explained Mr. Alloway, "and with only two or three boys. I hear it said all the time that boys these days can't practice like their fathers did—no vacant lots they can turn into fields. But a vacant lot isn't necessary. Here, pitch to me easy and underhanded."

Mr. Alloway held the bat as if bunting. He punched the ball right back at Robin. It went between his legs.

"I never was much of an infielder," Robin explained lamely.

"You have to field ground balls at every position. Come on."

Another pitch. This time a line poke right at Robin's feet. He missed again.

"Don't worry," said Mr. Alloway. "It takes hours. And I can tell you this—when you master the pepper game you can play any position."

Robin speared the next one but his pitch was wild, going over Mr. Alloway's head.

"Now let's get this straight," his stepfather said with his first show of firmness. "You can't help not catching some of the hits. Even most of them. But you *can* pitch the ball accurately from ten feet away. Can't you?"

"Yes, sir," Robin confessed.

"Then there are only two explanations for throws like that, carelessness or getting in a hurry. You've taken piano lessons, haven't you?"

"Yes, sir."

"Well, throws like these are just like practicing your scales. You master pitches of ten or twelve feet, then the longer throws come easier. The main thing is to be careful every time you turn loose of the ball. You know something, our league statistician did some research this winter. He went over the league records for the last ten years. And do you know what those records show? Each year the championship team was the one which made the fewest throwing errors. Did you ever think of the game that way?"

"No, sir."

"That is how important it is, in Little League anyhow. Now you bat a while."

Robin held the bat as instructed, hands about three inches apart, the bottom set of fingers gripping tightly. He missed more pitches than he hit but Mr. Alloway seemed satisfied.

"You have a good eye," said the manager. "I noticed that in last year's tryouts. But you must move quicker, Robin."

Robin bit his lips and lowered his head so that Mr. Alloway would not see his expression.

His mother called from the doorway.

"Game called because of woman's edict," she said firmly. "I refuse to let baseball interfere with our meal schedule."

"Point conceded for the present," Mr. Alloway said with a grin. "But I warn the opposition of a future filibuster."

The dinner was tasty—chicken, mashed potatoes, green peas. But Mrs. Alloway realized quickly that she had not prepared enough.

"Lead me to the gallows," she offered as she regarded two emptied plates and two unsatisfied expressions. "I am having to learn about buying groceries again. I never saw a full-grown man eat more than you do, Chase. And Robin is taking right after you."

"Maybe you never fed him enough in the first place." His voice, as it usually did, had a teasing quality which took the sting out of his words. "He might be bigger if you had."

"He weighs enough for his age and height."

"Who said so?"

"Dr. Anderson. Robin has regular checkups. And I am sure the doctors are correct."

"I am sure of that, too. But Dr. Anderson isn't measuring boys for sports. If they breathe and can walk, he is satisfied. We set higher standards in my league. What do you weigh, Robin?"

"About eighty-five pounds."

"Not enough. You'll be knocking at a hundred and ten when you're twelve."

"He might," conceded Mrs. Alloway, "if he keeps up his exercise and his appetite. How is your baseball coming along, Robin?"

"Fine. Mr. Alloway is teaching me a lot."

Mr. Alloway leaned back in his chair. "I see no reason to postpone this family crisis any longer," he declared. "I will not be *Mister* Alloway in my house, or rather the one my wife lets me live in. My players don't even call me *Mister* Alloway, none except the new ones."

"You can see Robin's position, dear," Mrs. Alloway said quickly. "He has been taught to address every grown man as mister. And until he gets used to you— this was not his doing, you know, but ours."

"I understand," was the quick answer. "I am not Robin's real father. I don't expect him to think of me as such. But the mister business!"

"What do you want him to call you?" There was anxiety in her voice. Robin himself listened tight-lipped, and troubled, very troubled. He certainly did not want to be the subject of friction between his mother and stepfather. Mr. Alloway was making his mother happier. Robin, too—it thrilled him every afternoon to come home and find his mother waiting for him with a smile instead of the way it had been since his father's death.

Mr. Alloway was serious, too; no question of it. "I don't know," he said slowly. "I cannot have proved too much in so short a time. Nor do I expect anything so important taken for granted. But, Robin, haven't I convinced you that I am at least a friend?"

"Yes, sir," gulped Robin. He wanted to add more, but the words choked in his throat.

"Then at least call me Chase. Two-thirds of the boys do that anyhow."

"Yes, sir," Robin said quickly. And gratefully, for he wanted the subject closed. He hoped he never had to explain his feelings. He was becoming fonder of Chase Alloway every day. But he was prejudiced against the word stepfather. That could be due to some books he had read in which the stepfathers were inconsiderate or cruel, or indifferent at the least. A close friend was more desirable than a stepfather.

"I told you," Mark said the next day. "You'll make a team all right, with a manager for a stepfather. Mr. Alloway will teach you so much you can't *help* but be good enough."

"Sure," Dave said enviously. "He'll take you any-how."

"He hasn't taught me much so far," Robin said rue-fully. "And he sure hasn't said anything about taking me on his team."

Mark and Dave were his only close friends. A change had come over Robin's personality after his father's ac-cident; he knew so because of talk overheard between his mother and Dr. Edward Haines. Mrs. Scott had in-sisted on the psychiatric treatments. Robin had gone unwillingly. Dr. Haines had voiced some phrases in Latin, Greek or something. Their meaning, according to his mother, was that Robin resented the loss of his father and so avoided close association with other boys. The explanation made no sense at all to him; he felt that his mother had wasted both time and money on Dr. Haines. If the psychiatrist was right, then why did he spend so much time with Mark and Dave?

"Besides," Robin said firmly, "I don't want him just *taking* me on his team. If I can make it——"

"You're a chump," Dave said. "I'll take a major league uniform any way I can get it, even if I just sit in the dugout."

"Both of you ought to make it this year. You did well in the minor league. Mr. Carowe said so."

"Sure, Mr. Carowe," grunted Mark. "He doesn't know anything about coaching; he said so himself. He just took the team because nobody else would."

"I guess you think if you had a manager for a stepfather—well, I'll tell you what. I'll ask Chase tonight if he will help you, too."

"You call him by his first name?"

"He wants me to," shrugged Robin. "He said all the boys on his team do."

"Maybe on his team," said Dave. "But not on the Giants. Everybody on that team says Mister Tracy."

"He's older than Chase."

"Harder on his boys, too," added Mark. "I've heard that's why your stepdad never has won a championship. He isn't tough enough."

That could be true, decided Robin. Chase did not seem to be a stern man.

"Do you want him to help you or not?" Robin demanded. "If you don't, quit whining about how lucky I am."

"Sure we want his help. Don't you forget to ask him tonight."

Robin did not forget. He made his proposal at the dinner table.

"Two of my friends want to practice with us," he said hesitantly. He was still not accustomed to Chase's presence at the table or in the den. "Mark Kelly and Dave Presley."

"I know them," nodded Mr. Alloway. "They came very near to making the league last year. I was thinking about Mark myself, and then—well, player auctions don't always go the way you want them to. I ended up with a boy I hadn't planned to take."

"I thought managers chose their own boys," put in Robin's mother.

"Not exactly. The managers bid on the boys. And you must pretend an interest sometimes. You want the other coaches to spend their points. If Jim or Sneaker really wants a boy—well, you must see that they pay a good price."

"It sounds to me like a modern version of the slave market."

"It is, sort of." The tall man smiled. "But we never beat the boys or sell them downriver to the sugar plantations. Dave and Mark seem to be fine boys. Tell them to come over and play with us any time. And if they want to take conditioning drills with you, that's all right, too."

Robin looked his surprise. Conditioning drills? What did Chase mean?

"You react too slowly," Chase said, almost impersonally. "You are not agile enough to play any position. Your legs are weak. You need wind sprints. And the way to teach a boy agility—make a catcher out of him. We will get started on a lot of things in a day or two."

Robin stared at his stepfather, who now was intent on his dessert apparently feeling that no further conversation was needed. Didn't Chase know about the automobile accident which had taken Roger Scott's life and sent Robin to the hospital? Robin licked his lips. Should he tell Chase what had happened? He decided against it. His mother could tell him, and make sure Robin was not around when she explained. For Robin did not want to offer his own excuses. He did not want Chase thinking—well, his mother could do his alibiing better than he could.

Dave and Mark were in Robin's back yard the next day as soon as they could get parental permission and find their gloves. Chase had given directions for them to play simple catch until he could get home. If you want to be a ball player, play catch day and night; so he had told his stepson. You don't ever get enough easy tossing, not even in the big leagues.

"Hi," Chase said informally as he stepped into the back yard.

"Hello, Mr. Alloway," Mark and Dave said in unison.

"Keep on throwing," he said. "I want to build a little gadget first."

He took several pieces of stripping out of the car, set up two triangular shaped stands, then drove small nails into each.

"Gosh, Mr. Alloway," said Mark, "that looks like the start of a jumping pit."

"Three feet high!" Dave snorted scornfully.

"That's exactly what it is, a jumping pit. Or maybe a springing pit is a better description."

He finished and gestured for them to sit down. "This will make sense later," he said, pointing to his contraption. "Right now let us settle one point. Robin says you want me to help you."

"Yes, sir."

"I will, as much as league rules allow. That limits us to this yard. Robin I can take out to the field. I am setting one solid requirement, though. I don't care how sorry or how good you are now, but you must improve. You must show me, and keep showing me, that I *am* helping you."

"We will, Mr. Alloway," Mark said eagerly.

"All right, let's take the first sure test. Mark, from how far back can you clear this bar, springing off your left foot?"

Mark hesitated, appraised the standard an instant, then cleared it from a full yard away. Chase took out a metal ruler and recorded the distance.

"Good," the manager approved. "Very good, in fact. Show that spring in tryouts, plus some throwing and catching, and you'll end up on a major team. Your turn, Dave."

"I can't spring like Mark," Dave confessed.

"I told you, I don't care what you can do now. I just want you to be doing a little better every day. Do what you can."

Dave settled on fourteen inches or so. His mark went into the record, too.

"All right, Robin. Your turn."

Robin's lips tightened. He was sure that he could not clear the barrier at all, not springing off his left foot.

"Let me try the right foot."

"No," Chase said firmly. "Same rules for everybody."

Robin tried. The cross piece clattered to the turf.

"Don't worry about it," Chase said calmly. "Now how about some pepper?"

He used the bat first. Both Mark and Dave were as

inept as Robin. The ball came so quickly, complained Mark. Couldn't Mr. Alloway stand back a little farther? He shook his head. He was a volunteer little league manager, he explained, not a paid babysitter. If they weren't asking his help because they wanted a uniform, then they were wasting their time and his.

"Yes, sir," panted Dave, "that is what we're hoping for. But we're looking like—well, clucks."

"I agree," Chase said calmly. "What do you expect, to get to be major leaguers in ten minutes? Maybe that is why you were left behind in the minors last year while twenty-four of your group moved up."

He turned the bat over to Robin, who drew some compliments but more criticism.

"You hold the bat level," he said again. "Bend your knees instead of lowering the bat."

Mark and Dave fared even worse. Neither seemed to know the first principles of bunting and dragging.

"You had better learn by April 2 if you want to move up," Chase told them coldly. "That is, unless you are home run hitters."

"I hit three last year," Mark said proudly.

Chase shook his head. "That isn't enough. If a boy can hit six hundred and put the ball out of the park every game, I'll play him even if he has two left feet. But any other boy has to play the game *my* way."

Throwing next. Chase brought out a worn catcher's mitt.

"This is for you," he said to his stepson.

"Me!" His stepfather had mentioned trying him as a

catcher but Robin had not taken that seriously. He was not even sure how to put the mitt on, and said so.

"Just one way, unless you try it on the wrong hand. Now crouch in the catcher's position. Like this."

Robin did his best to imitate his stepfather. It wasn't easy but he gritted his teeth and did it. Meanwhile Mr. Alloway corrected the throwing motions of Mark and Dave. Either three-quarters or overhanded, he said. The underhanded tosses are fine for second basemen or shortstops, after they learn other fundamentals of the positions.

Shift with the pitch! Move your body! Catch the pitch off the chest! Robin tried until his leg almost collapsed under him. But he refused even to consider quitting. His mother must make his alibi. He had decided that and he would not relent regardless of what happened.

Finally Chase called a halt.

"Come back tomorrow if you want to," he told Mark and Dave casually. "Rob and I will be at it again, unless I'm tied up at the office."

The "Rob" brought a grin to the weary boy's face. His father had always called him that, but not many other people. He preferred the abbreviation. He knew girls named Robin, but none named Rob.

"We'll come back if we can, Mr. Alloway," Mark spoke for both of them. "Our parents may not let us, and we're having homework piled up on us. But if we can—and thanks a lot."

Robin limped into the house.

"Get hit by a ball?" asked his stepfather.

Robin did not answer immediately. "Nothing special," he said finally. "Just tired, I suppose."

"Sure," Chase nodded. "Take a hot bath. Rub alcohol into any soreness. But if your arm hurts, be sure and tell me."

Robin shook his head. It wasn't his arm; that never bothered him. He lowered his head under his mother's anxious look. She knew what was paining him.

"You must be thirsty," she said. "How about a soda pop?"

"The coach is tired, too," Chase said lightly, sitting on the kitchen stool. "Any chance of some iced tea?"

His mother prepared both drinks. "You had quite a session," she remarked. Robin detected the different tone in her voice if his stepfather didn't.

"Just a starter," he said. "There's a lot to be done—for Mark and Dave as well as Robin."

"Maybe," she suggested, "it isn't that important to them. I am no judge of such things; I'll be the first to admit that. But it seemed to me you were *working* them rather than playing with them."

He nodded. "You have your point. It comes up with every boy every year. That is why we divide Little League into three classifications—the majors, the minors and the teams for boys eight and nine years old."

He took a sip of his tea before going on. "I don't contend that every boy should play all-out Little League baseball any more than I say every youngster should learn to play a musical instrument. We must develop more than baseball players out of this generation. But I know how strong the competition is for the major league. There will be two hundred boys out; twenty will get uniforms. If Robin doesn't want me to help him——?"

He spoke up for himself. "I do. I sure do. So do Mark and Dave."

"I think so," nodded Chase. "I just wish we had more space."

"Why can't you use the regular field?"

"The league forbids that. A coach cannot hold anything like a regular practice before the season officially opens."

"He can't even help his own stepson?"

"Certainly, and I am trying. But we cannot use league facilities."

"Mr. Kelly has a bigger yard than ours," Robin volunteered. "Let me ask him about it."

"Go ahead."

The boy hurried to the telephone. "Mr. Kelly? . . . Rob Scott (no more Robin for him) . . . my stepfather is helping . . . yes, that's Chase Alloway . . . Mark and Dave and me . . . we want to make a major league team this year . . . yes, sir, that's how we feel. We ought to forget about it if we don't make it this year. . . . Can we practice in your side yard? . . . No, sir, we won't tear up your shrubbery. . . . Thank you, sir. If we are hurting anything, then we'll quit. . . . Yes, sir. Thank you again, Mr. Kelly."

He returned to the breakfast table, face beaming. He had done something himself.

"I would say, Rob, that you have possibilities as a salesman," Chase said drily. "Where is this new scene of our crime?"

"Just a block from here, 2806 Bonnie Road."

"I'll come up there as soon as I can," promised his stepfather. "Don't do anything but play easy catch until I get there."

Mark and Dave protested that order, but Rob was able to subdue them. "He doesn't have to help us, you know. And we aren't boys who have made the major league; we are three clucks who flopped. We've *got* to make it this year. So let's do just what he says."

The Kelly yard was considerably more spacious than the Scott lawn. No flower beds, either, just elm trees and ornamental shrubs. Mr. Kelly arrived just after Chase.

"Mighty nice of you to do this, Mr. Alloway," he said, holding out his hand. "I just hope something comes of it."

"Something might," Chase said lightly. "We'll do as little damage to your yard as possible."

"Forget the grass," said Mr. Kelly. "I can't make carpet grass grow under these elms anyway. The shrubs, yes, particularly the gardenias and crepe myrtles. They are the only things on the place worth keeping alive."

"In that case," Chase said, "we might do some hitting."

"Go ahead," shrugged the portly owner.

Chase began as on other days, with a brisk pepper game. He turned hitting over to Rob and put on a glove himself. He fielded the first pitch neatly and feinted a pitch right back. But instead he flipped the ball behind him to Dave. The boy was caught completely unprepared. Both Rob and Mark giggled at the victim's rueful expression.

"I am not playing tricks," explained the manager. "Let's all four work on this clowning business. Did you boys ever consider that circus stars must be among the best athletes in the world? Look at their agility, their quick reflexes, their alertness. That is why I am starting this foolishness. We'll look silly ar first, of course, but golly, remember our first pepper game."

"You mean look one way and throw another?" asked Dave.

"Some of the time. Don't settle on any routine. Let's be tricky often enough to keep the other two on their toes, watching every move out of the corner of one eye. The sports writers call that split vision and claim it is a natural gift. To an extent it may be, but I believe much of it is developed by long practice. Besides, it is fun, isn't it?"

All three boys agreed. "You get in the act at batting, Rob. Learn to look one way but hit in another direction."

Rob's first effort was a miserable failure. He retrieved the ball disgustedly.

"I don't see how anybody can do that," he complained.

"Paul Waner could," the coach said. "The old timers said Willie Keeler could, too. I don't know about him; I never saw him play. But I did see Waner do it time after time. He led the league in hitting and he couldn't power the ball three hundred feet on a still day. But let's don't worry about our misses. We are doing this to laugh at each other. And, Rob, you thought it quite funny when Dave was the dunce."

Rob had to concede that. But he was grateful when it was Mark's turn to bat. Temporarily, that is. He proved an easy victim of almost any throwing duplicity. He brooded over his showing as Mr. Alloway allowed them a drink and a short rest. Mark and Dave were improving more than he, no doubt of that. Rob rubbed his left leg and bit his lips. It wasn't fair, he whispered to himself. How could he compete on even terms with his friends?

Pitching again, Rob with the mitt. He squatted according to his stepfather's directions. He had to; Chase never took an eye off him. The manager seemed more concerned with Rob's catching than with the hurling efforts of Dave and Mark.

Keep his weight even—how could he do that? He could sort of lean on his right knee and do a creditable job of receiving, better than he had believed he could. He had never wanted to be a catcher anyhow. His choice was first base, where he had played as a minor leaguer, where there was not so much pressure on his left leg.

"Let me try pitching," he proposed.

Chase refused. "You are right where you belong, for

the time being. And quit that right knee business. The next time I see you doing it, a lap around the field."

That happened three throws later. Rob circled the yard dutifully, and also painfully. Resentfully, too. Why didn't Chase talk like that to Dave and Mark? Rob remembered what Ed Warren had told him. Ed's father was assistant manager of the Calumet Cats. "It is ten times harder to play under your dad than anybody else," Ed had complained. "I never do anything right. And every time I stop to breathe—it's Warren, take another lap."

Was that happening to him, brooded Rob. Would he be the goat of every workout, even these informal practices? Maybe, he mused, that was the difference between a father and a stepfather. He could remember his own father acting and speaking as if his son were the finest boy in the world. His stepfather corrected him at every turn—if there were other boys around. At home, sure, oh, sure, he was all concern and gentle banter. Chase had his mother wrapped around his little finger.

"Why don't you make the other boys take laps?" Robin asked finally. He could not resist it.

"Because they are trying their best to do what I tell them," Chase said evenly. "You are not. You are leaning on your right knee every time I turn my head. But let's get on with our practice. I believe we have room here for some outfield."

He took the bat and gestured them to spread out over the Kelly yard. The elms stopped some of his flies but not all. Their fly catching was as sloppy as had been their first pepper drill. Mark and Dave missed half of theirs, Rob caught only one. But, noticed Rob, his chances were more difficult than those of his friends. Chase never hit the ball *to* him, always just out of his reach. His one catch had come only after a desperate dive.

That night Rob brooded about his plight until he fell asleep from sheer fatigue. What could an eleven-year-old boy do? He wanted his mother to be happy; obviously she adored Chase Alloway. So had Rob himself, until this baseball business started. That was it, he finally decided. He could not please his stepfather as a ball player; he simply lacked the physical ability. He rubbed his left leg, which was hurting him, and had both nights. Chase did not realize the pain he inflicted, of course; he did not know that he was demanding full performance from a handicapped boy. I must tell him, Robin decided. Or should his mother do that for him? She would, of course. She was concerned already; she showed it. Let her tell Chase. Robin finally fell asleep with that decision.

CHAPTER 3

Chase Wins His Point

R<small>OBIN SAID NOTHING</small> to his mother until Chase had left, then said he must talk to her even if it meant being tardy to school.

She nodded. "If it is that serious, let's have it. I thought everything was going smoothly."

He sighed, wishing his mother knew more about baseball. "It's—it's practice."

"What about practice? You said you wanted your stepfather to help you. Your friends, too."

"Yes, Mother. And he *is* helping us." Robin had trouble choosing his words. "Mark and Dave are sure learning, too. They'll make the league this year. But——"

"You won't? Or you *think* you won't?"

Robin's eyes brimmed with tears. "Chase wants me to catch. He makes me crouch like this——"

And he showed her, wincing at the throb of pain in the calf of his leg.

His mother understood at once. "And that hurts, doesn't it?"

"It sure does," Robin confessed. "It hurts all the time."

"Have you ever told Chase about your leg or showed it to him?"

"No, Mom. I didn't want to—well, alibi. I want to keep up with the boys. You can understand that."

She shook her blonde head. "That is not exactly true, Robin. You have never been very friendly with the more athletic boys. You have stuck close to Mark and Dave. Why? Because they do not surpass you—at least not so much?"

"Gosh, no. We just get along, that's all."

Mrs. Alloway studied her son an instant, then said gently, "We'll discuss this tonight. I will not have Chase overtaxing you. If he cannot understand the situation, then we must . . . well, let's consider that later. And if your leg is paining you so much, then stay in bed all day."

"You mean I can miss school?"

"Yes," his mother said wearily. "We have a more important matter to settle."

The day passed slowly for Robin. He read, watched television and once fell asleep for a short time. But his conscience kept plaguing him. Somehow, someway, he should have avoided this situation. His brooding took in both sides, more his than his stepfather's, of course; but he considered Chase's viewpoint, too. There was no doubting that Chase wanted to help him, and Dave and Mark, too. The latter were enjoying every minute of the special drills. They claimed at school that Mr. Alloway topped Jim Tracy as a manager. Not many West Austin boys would agree. Mr. Tracy's teams had won the championship for five consecutive seasons. It wasn't easy to dispute success like that.

Maybe his mother could arrange some sort of compromise. If only Chase would consider that left leg and let up on drills, especially that catching. That crouching caused most of his pain. The pepper games, now— Rob could not help grinning. He was learning some tricks of his own. Yesterday he had bounced the ball off his shoulder right into Mark's hands. Mark had been so astonished that he made no effort to catch the ball.

He didn't really want to quit, mused Rob. Chase *must* be made to understand. A boy so handicapped had small chance of playing in the major league. But in the minor loop—if Chase would keep helping him, realizing his deficiency, he could be the best first baseman in the secondary loop. He had hit an even three hundred the year before, even lacking the speed to beat out ground balls.

Would it have been better if he had reasoned with Chase himself? No, words would have failed him. His mother would do better, unless she lost her temper. She could be fierce in her championship of him.

Then Chase's car turned into the driveway and Robin

knew the showdown was almost at hand. He waited for the summons, and it came within minutes. His mother and stepfather sat facing each other, Chase sipping iced tea as usual.

"Now what is this crisis confronting us?" His tone was calm, his eyes twinkling.

"There need be no crisis at all," Mrs. Alloway said, struggling to match her husband's casual manner. "I am sure that after you know about Robin's bad left leg ——"

"I do know about it," Chase broke in. "I knew that before I ever had a date with you."

This casualness startled Robin. Also his mother, he noticed. Her eyes went wide.

"How did you know? I don't remember telling you."

"Robin suffered some bad burns on his cheek, neck and shoulder," Chase went on. "The surgeon had to graft skin from his left leg not once, but several times. The awful business took months and interfered with his use of his leg. He has favored it ever since. It pains him after a little effort."

"But who told ——?"

"I don't remember," Chase said with a shrug. "I didn't learn it as a curious suitor, but as a Little League manager. Rob hit well in the tryouts last year but moved awkwardly. I wondered why—if he was lazy or just didn't have coordination—and found out."

Mrs. Alloway was speechless for a moment. "Do you find out—such things—about all the boys who try out?"

Chase grinned. "I know; you mothers believe we can't hold a fair tryout in two days. And we couldn't without our scouts."

"What scouts?"

"The boys who played for us last year. Come to try-outs this year and see how it's done."

She shook her head. "I wouldn't understand what I saw. I am no baseball fan." She took a deep breath. "Nor can I understand," she said in a sterner tone, "why you don't consider Robin's leg in your so called practices?"

Robin saw his stepfather's lips twitch. "I do," Chase said quietly.

"When it pains him so severely—to crouch like you tell him?"

"Yes."

Mrs. Alloway's lips trembled. "Robin probably never will use that leg very well, Chase. I have tried every-thing. I bought him an exercise trampoline. He has been to masseurs and physical therapists. The trainer from the University of Texas has treated him. Besides, isn't catching harder on the legs than any other posi-tion?"

"Yes, it is," said Chase, "especially when the catcher crouches properly. When Robin can do that without much pain, then ——"

He shrugged his shoulders. Robin noticed the change in his mother's expression, especially her eyes, which gleamed brighter than usual.

"Then this is your version of—well, special treatment?"

"You can call it that." He sighed, then smiled again. "You two have brought up the subject, so now you have to listen. I see that neither of you know the story of one Chase Alloway."

"What story?"

"My last college football season."

"You were a famous player, I know that." Robin nodded to show that he was aware of his stepfather's record, too.

"And you are an amazing physical specimen for your age," his wife put in. "I was rather shocked to learn that you are forty-three."

Robin could not help gasping. Forty-three? Impossible.

"Thank you," Chase said. He hesitated. "You also know I hold the Purple Heart."

"Yes. You were hit by shrapnel."

Robin's eyes widened. He had not known of this.

"Hit in the arm, my passing arm," Chase said tersely. "Almost tore it off. The surgeon sewed it back together but said I would never make much use of it again. Dead nerves, he said, as well as torn muscles."

He paused. "I couldn't believe him. I didn't *dare* to. I had to use this arm to play football again. I had to play football because I needed a scholarship. The surgeon said I might try squeezing a rubber ball and other exercises. He brought me one. I could use two fingers then. A week later I could move all five. The doctor rigged me up a sort of pulley. I couldn't reach it at first. Then I couldn't hold on to it. Finally I made it. Then I used bar bells a while. I tried to throw a football and I was like a girl."

He licked his lips and looked down at the floor. "There are college record books to tell you the rest."

Robin looked to see his mother's reactions. He saw tears in her eyes, but he also observed her smile.

"I am no football fan either, but I believe I know the rest," she said slowly. "Chase Alloway made All-American his senior year in college."

"Golly!" exclaimed Robin. "Did you pass a lot?"

"Yes," said Chase. "But let's play down this All-American stuff. I made one selection, just one. But this old arm I'd never use again passed my team to a championship and that's what counted." He paused. "I see no reason to give up on Robin at the age of eleven," he added. "He is partly my responsibility, too."

"Yes," Mrs. Alloway agreed, "he is." Her lips trembled. "I suppose I've been weak, like all mothers. The exercises hurt Robin so; I couldn't force him to continue. And, of course, he was too young to see the full picture himself. You could. And if he *wants* to play Little League baseball bad enough ——"

"He has weaknesses to correct," Chase said. "He hit over three hundred in the minor league but was weak on pegs to his right. He couldn't come off the bag properly nor would he stretch with his weight on his left foot. The balls he let go hurt his team, cost the Cougars the title, in fact."

"Is he improving, really improving now, Chase? He *must* feel some sense of accomplishment, receive some encouragement ——"

"I am not satisfied with him," Chase said with a sigh. "But I have another little trick up my sleeve. Rob, can you wait for me after school tomorrow?"

"Yes, sir."

"What this time?" His mother's tone was gentle.

"Just something else to try," Chase said. "And if it doesn't help ——"

"You never give up, do you?"

He chuckled. "I am still trying to win a West Austin Little League championship, and I still think I will— some day. And what if I did give up easily? You told me positively that you would never marry again, and I didn't give up on that either."

"I surrender," Mrs. Alloway said mildly. "What about you, Robin? Do you really *want* to accept Chase's training?"

Robin's answer was slow in coming. At last he said, "I want to play Little League baseball—in the major league. And I did miss a bunch of balls at first base last season."

"Shall we collect Mark and Dave and have another go at it?"

"Yes, sir," Robin said quickly.

Chase was waiting when Robin came out of the school building. "Where are we going?" he asked curiously as his stepfather turned right on Enfield Road, toward the business district.

"To see an orthopedic specialist, Dr. Anton Wukasch. You won't understand half he says, but you'll like him. I have an idea, but I want his approval."

Robin was further surprised when Chase took an old shin guard out of his car. "What's that for?" he asked.

"Maybe for you, if Dr. Wukasch agrees."

Dr. Wukasch was a small, ruddy-faced man with a white goatee. He listened gravely as Chase explained about Robin's burns and the unsuccessful treatments of his leg. Then he ordered Robin up on his examining table.

"The skin, she is doing fine," the German declared. "But the right leg, it is better developed. With a growing boy, a leg weight should do the trick. And exercise, of course, much exercise."

"What about baseball, Doctor?"

"Running, jumping—all of it." Dr. Wukasch stroked his goatee. "But what sort of weight? I ——"

"How about this, Doctor?"

Chase handed over the shin guard. The specialist chuckled.

"Won't it work?"

"It should." The doctor put the guard on Robin's leg. "It is too long. I will trim it."

"Yes."

The doctor worked swiftly. "There," he said proudly. "Try it. How does it feel, lad?"

Robin grimaced as he clomped about. "Like a shin guard," he said at once.

"It will do," Dr. Wukasch declared. "If he will walk and run ——"

"In this!" exclaimed Robin.

"Of course. It is the wearing and the exercises ——"

Tears welled in Robin's eyes. "I'll . . . I'll look like a . . . golly, a freak. You mean to school and ——!"

"Yes," Chase said gently.

"But you don't know those smart alecks at school!"

"I think I do," Chase said. "Oh, they will make fun of you at first. I faced the same thing, partner." A smile touched his lips. "You should have heard those wise guys in the hospital when I said I was going to throw a football again." The smile left as suddenly as it had appeared. "But my first game after I got back—the sports writers made a little fuss over my starting at quarterback. You should have seen the telegrams, Rob—some from men still bedbound in hospitals, men I had never even met."

Rob bit his lip. "Sure. You were a star."

"I wasn't born that way. But if the kids poking fun at you ——"

"It is nothing," Dr. Wukasch put in. "But if you do not have the heart ——"

Rob's lips trembled. He had already decided. There was, after all, only one choice. He would wear the silly shin guard. But his stepfather and Dr. Wukasch were wrong about how his classmates would react. They liked to tease him anyway. The bigger boys—Bruce Elliott, Bill Roberts and Joe Pittman—never missed a chance to humiliate him.

The fact that his mother must splice his blue jeans with extra cloth did not help either.

"Hey, Scott. Your breeches are torn!"

"What's the shin guard for, Scott?"

"Don't you know? His stepfather is a manager, so Robin can wear the castoff equipment!"

"Sure. Remember when you were a little kid? I put on my brother's old uniform every chance I got. The breeches flopped down to my shoes, but I didn't care. I thought I looked cute!"

And Mr. Cully, the physical education teacher, questioned him before the whole class.

"Robin, how can you take calisthenics in that shin guard?"

Gene Meador answered. "He's just as clumsy without it, Mr. Cully. It won't make any difference."

"That's enough, Gene. Why are you wearing it, Robin?"

Robin licked his dry lips, then managed an answer. "The doctor said to, Mr. Cully. My left leg isn't as strong as my right and a half-inch shorter."

Mr. Cully doubled as assistant coach of the eighth grade football team; he appreciated the value of the shin guard at once.

"That's a good idea, Robin. And I won't make P.T.

any easier for you because of it. That would hold back your development."

"Yes, sir."

He received some sympathy from the lady teachers. "Do you want to leave a minute early, Robin?" White-haired Miss Dorcas asked the question. "I don't want you late for your next class."

"If you get deals like that," spoke up Dick Flanagan, "I'm going to wear my shin guards. Both of them."

Miss Dorcas voiced quick reproof but could not stop the chorus of titters.

Outside after class, Curt Cooley called to Dick, who was catcher for the Dodgers, "Don't figure on making the all-star team this year, Flanagan. Scott is getting the jump on you."

"He'll never beat me out," boasted Dick, "even if his new stepfather is a manager."

"He's one vote ahead of you right now," teased Curt. He and Flanagan formed the Bedford Dodgers' ace bat-tery.

"Scott isn't even in the league yet. And he won't be, unless his stepfather takes him."

Robin clomped home; he had refused his mother's offer to come for him. It was only eight blocks, but that half-mile seemed an impossible distance this day, es-pecially when he walked blindly some of the distance, unable to keep tears out of his eyes.

Finally he reached the front door. His mother was starting for the grocery store but changed her mind when she saw her son's expression.

"Was it a bad day, dear?"

"Yes, ma'am." Tears came again. "They made fun of me all day," he sobbed. "I knew they would. I told Chase so."

"He knew it, too," Mrs. Alloway said comfortingly. "Do you know what he told me just before he left for the office?"

"What?"

"He said this would be a bitter day for you, maybe the worst you've had—since the accident. I'll tell you his exact words—'one of the longest miles he'll ever walk.' He said he would give a thousand dollars if he could walk it for you."

The tears suddenly stopped. All but one hurt suddenly lost their importance.

"Mom, make him promise one thing. And I mean for sure."

"What is it, honey?"

Dick Flanagan's scornful words had rung in Robin's ears for the past two hours. *Scott isn't even in the league. And he won't be unless his stepfather takes him!*

"I don't want him taking me on his team just because ——"

Mrs. Alloway pressed her cheek against Robin's. "I understand, dear. It would only make things worse for you among your friends."

"I don't have any friends," Robin said hoarsely. "Not even Mark and Dave any more. They made fun of me, too."

"You don't mean that, honey."

"I sure do. I don't want to play with them today."

But Chase changed Robin's mind about that.

"We can't let personalities interfere with Little League baseball," he said firmly. "What happens off the field can't be carried *onto* the field. We need Dave and Mark to have any sort of practice."

Robin hung his head and nodded. "Yes, sir." Then he looked up hopefully. "Do I have to catch again?"

"Certainly. You catch every day until a week before practice begins. Then I'll turn you loose."

"What do you mean, turn me loose?"

"You can try just about anything, and I can see how much you have improved."

CHAPTER 4

An Unexpected Assist

Rᴏʙɪɴ ᴡᴀꜱ ꜱᴜʀᴘʀɪꜱᴇᴅ at how quickly he adjusted to the cumbersome shin guard. Three days after he donned it, he walked and ran as if he had borne the handicap since infancy. He could even participate in the pepper games without falling. They were a tricky trio by now, with tosses between their legs, behind their backs, off their shoulders—sometimes, when batting, Robin lost track of the ball himself. Dave and Mark progressed as fly catchers, too; they could catch nearly any fly ball that cleared the elms. Robin could not match them, of course, and Chase continued to hit flys just out of his reach. His stepfather, Robin decided, used a fungo bat as skillfully as a conductor wielded a baton. Chase could hit a spinning drive deliberately, and those were almost impossible to hold. One must not only reach and grab the ball; he must also squeeze it tightly.

Robin's schoolmates paid less and less attention to the shin guard, too. All but Dick Flanagan, that is. The Dodger catcher persisted with his taunts. Finally Robin could endure no more. He challenged Dick during recess.

"Take off that guard," snapped Dick, "and I'll show you a trick or two. I can't fight you with it on and you know it."

"Why not?"

"You know why. I won't take that advantage of you."

"I get around with it pretty well," Robin said coldly.

Mr. Cully came around the school building just then and broke up the quarrel. Both boys went to the principal's office. Dick was sullen and refused any explanation. Robin decided to take the same attitude, except politely. Just an argument, he said. Both were equally at fault.

The principal, Henry Robbins, lifted his eyebrows.

"You were willing to fight Dick despite that shin guard?"

"Yes, sir."

"Dick outweighs you twenty pounds, Robin."

Robin recalled Dr. Wukasch's words—flesh and bone meant nothing, only the heart.

"That doesn't mean he can whip me," he said grimly.

"No," conceded Mr. Robbins, "it doesn't." He turned to Dick. "Can you quit teasing Robin every time he walks down the hall?"

"Yes, sir," the bigger boy said promptly. "I'd better,"

he added cheerfully. "I'll have a scrap on my hands if I don't."

"Then shake hands and let's forget it," said the principal.

Robin recreated every word and gesture as he walked home. He had offered to fight Dick Flanagan, even with his shin guard! Mark overtook him.

"What's this about you standing up to Dick?" he asked at once.

"Oh, nothing."

"Did you or didn't you?" Mark persisted.

"Who told you about it?"

"Dick himself. He told it all over school. He says you won't back down before anybody." Mark's voice held both awe and pride.

"I'm not saying anything like that," Robin answered quickly.

"Dick said he should have known you have guts, that anybody who'd wear a shin guard to build up his weak leg would have."

Dave intercepted them at the corner of Enfield and Exposition. He was excited, too, and had something new to add to Mark's report.

"You sure got Dick Flanagan on your side in a hurry. He said he hoped you got on the Dodgers because you'll be a ball player next year."

"It'll be next year before I make it," Robin said with a sigh. "You two stand a good chance this season."

"Won't you get on your stepfather's team automatically? Most boys whose dads are managers ——"

"He is not my father," Robin said.

"But he's your stepfather," Mark argued. "That ought to make you an option player. Surely the league won't object to that."

"I am not going to the tryouts as an option player," Robin said firmly. "That is settled already."

And so it had been. Robin had managed to overhear most of the talk between his mother and Chase.

"Robin asked me to discuss this with you. He does not want to be taken on your team just because he is your stepson," Janet Alloway had said.

Chase frowned. "I am not sure that he will be considered an option player anyhow."

"What is an option player?"

"A coach may take his son at a regular price—a thousand points in our league. And a boy with an older brother already on a team goes at the same terms," he explained.

"Robin does not want that. He would rather play in the minor league another year."

"He may have no choice. The players' agent and the president rule on option players, not the managers."

"They *cannot* rule him your son, Chase."

Chase did not answer for an instant. Then he said, an unusual tone in his voice, "No, they can't do that, not against our wishes."

"Don't be hurt, dear. Robin is growing very fond of you. And you have already accomplished so much with him."

"I'm not hurt, honey. But I can wish he were really

my son, can't I? Whether that's right or wrong, I can't help it."

"You darling!"

Robin listened no more. It seemed to him that every talk about him ended with his mother kissing Chase or vice versa. Well, he mused as he slipped into bed—he did not want them to suspect that he had been eavesdropping—he could not blame Chase for the way he felt about her. It made no sense at all, but his mother got prettier every day.

Robin came to the breakfast table as usual. Chase was sipping coffee and reading the sports section. Robin took his usual place.

"Aren't you forgetting something?"

Robin looked blankly at his stepfather.

"Tryouts are one week from today," Chase said. "You can take off that shin guard."

"Will I have to put it back on after the tryouts?"

"I hope not. But we can't tell until we see how you move around. If you still favor that leg ——"

"I've been trying not to."

"I know you have. We will see this afternoon. By the way, the league will let me practice you at the park today."

"Mark and Dave, too?"

"No. The rules still hold; this is just one exception. I want to time you on circling the bases and a few other details."

"How did you swing the special permission?"

"I didn't," Chase said quietly. "The league president offered it." He took another sip of his coffee. "Fighters look around all of a sudden and find they have some surprising friends. How are things going at school?"

"Why, great." Robin was taken back by his father's explanation of the president's offer. But, now that he thought about it, he had better relations with his schoolmates than ever. More boys were stopping to talk with him. Girls, too.

"Improved, aren't they?"

"Yes, sir, they sure are." He hesitated. "Two or three talked to me yesterday. They have a fool idea I should run for vice-president of the class."

"What did you say?"

"I said I wasn't interested. I don't care who is vice-president, or if they even have one."

"But didn't you appreciate being asked?"

"Well, to tell the truth, I didn't think anything about it. I just grinned and walked off."

"I see." Chase rose from the table. "I had better scoot. Have on your running shoes today, partner. We'll soon find out if you are still a sidewheeler or if you have developed into a cabin cruiser." He stopped at the door. "I don't want to raise any false hopes, but Mac Collins might be at the park today, too. If he can't make it, I'm obligated to give him your base-running times and a full report on your fielding and hitting. Mac depends on his veterans to feed him information just as I do. It seems that his catcher reported you as a likely prospect."

"Yes, sir," mumbled Robin. "Dick Flanagan. I heard he was going to."

"I also heard the reason why. I didn't mention it to your mother, of course."

He was gone before Robin could recover his wits and voice his thanks. He sure did not want his mother to know that he had almost been involved in a fight on the school grounds. She might not understand such things.

The individual practice disappointed Robin. Oh, he moved more easily and a bit faster; he realized that at once. But he did not feel that there was any big difference. He trotted around the field twice, then raced the bases while Chase held a stop watch. Next he was drilled on sliding.

"Listen carefully and watch closely," Chase said. "You may never get another individual lesson. That is one of Little League's faults. Boys are sent sliding into bases without being taught how to slide. And leagues provide neither sliding pits nor pads. First, don't slide unless it's necessary. Too many boys like to show off. They think it's wonderful to hit the dirt. But, if it *is* going to be a close play, don't hesitate. Start about two steps away. Don't expect to slide directly into the bag. Come in opposite from the throw. Do you understand all this?"

Robin nodded. He thought he did. Then, turning to launch his run, he saw Dick Flanagan vaulting the fence. So did his stepfather. Chase called out to the Dodger catcher.

"Hi, Dick. Come give me a hand."

"Yes, sir." The red-haired boy came directly to Chase. "I'm glad to see you again, Mr. Alloway."

"Same to you, partner." Chase not only shook Dick's hand but squeezed his shoulder. "You've grown, darn it. You'll be even more trouble this year."

"I got a little fat around Christmas," Dick explained, "but I've run it off. I've worked on my throwing, too. You won't steal on me as much this season."

Robin watched and listened with mixed feelings. The cordiality surprised him at first. The major league teams played all out to win, no compulsory substitutions or anything like that. Games were usually close and hard-fought. But here the manager of the Winston Reds and the Dodger catcher talked like old friends. Plainly each respected the other. Then Robin realized what he was witnessing—courtesy between rivals, sportsmanship. He licked his lips. The day would come when opposing managers knew and treated him like this. And, he promised himself, he would respond just the way Dick had.

"Give me a hand," Chase said casually. "I'm trying to teach Rob how to slide. I'll cover second and you throw to me."

"From home plate?"

"Sure. That way you'll get some practice, too."

Dick's peg caught Robin two steps from the base. He slid but Chase slapped the ball against his leg.

"You came right into me," Chase scolded gently. "When you are caught dead, try to fake the baseman.

Feint one way and slide the other. Slide wide and try to hook the base."

"Yes, sir."

Another effort. This time Dick's peg was slightly to Chase's left. Robin remembered to slide in from a slight angle.

"You have the idea," Chase approved. "You almost made it. Probably no second baseman in the league would have gotten you out. I knew where to look for you, but then I've been at this a long time. Let's go again."

He called a halt ten minutes later. "We've had enough today. Thanks a lot, Dick."

"Sure, Mr. Alloway." The three of them were already at the water fountain, Robin drinking first. "The workout did me good, too. Robin—he can move better than I thought. He'll help your team next year for sure."

Robin almost choked as a swallow of water went down his windpipe. Dick was surprised by his speed! Did that mean he had improved more than he thought, or had Dick just considered him hopeless before?

"He isn't on my team yet, Dick. There are tryouts and then an auction. Remember?"

"But you can take him for ——"

"He won't be an option player, Dick."

Dick's surprised look went from Chase to Robin, then back again.

"Why not?"

"He isn't my son."

"But he's your ——"

"He doesn't *want* to be an option player. He doesn't want a uniform handed out to him because I married his mother."

Dick continued to look doubtful. "Can I tell that around? To Mac especially?"

"Robin will confirm it," Chase said lightly.

Robin nodded. A smile formed slowly on Dick's features. "That's cool, Scott," he approved. "That will go over good with the kids." The stocky catcher addressed Chase again. "All of us kids appreciate what you managers do, Mr. Alloway," he said slowly. "But some of us—most of us—don't see why a boy should be on a team just because of his dad. We've got to earn our uniform. Why shouldn't he?"

"I understand, Dick. If I had my way, there would be no option players in Little League. I don't like this having to take a little brother, either. Like Jim Holloway."

"Bob's little brother?"

"Yes."

"He's all right, Mr. Alloway. He horns in on games with Bob and the others at Tarrytown playground, and he holds his own pretty well. He may turn out to be better than Bob."

"I hope so. But he should have to win his uniform, as you did."

Dick nodded. "And like Rob will. So long, Mr. Alloway. I'll be seeing you, Rob."

Robin was speechless most of the way home. Then he blurted out: "I never thought I'd say that I liked Dick Flanagan."

Chase smiled. "That's the real good of Little League, partner," he said softly. "If it were just baseball, then it wouldn't be worth the trouble. But it brings boys together, welds new friendships, teaches strong loyalty. It does even more for adults, those who take it in the right spirit. Little League makes neighbors out of people who live close together but have been strangers before. It knits families tighter, too, makes parents pay more attention to the boys they have fed and clothed but might otherwise overlook in the hectic ways of our times."

Robin's lips twitched. He had never considered these things. Then he declared:

"Men like you—all managers—should get medals."

Chase shook his head. "Just the winners, partner. Why should we get any more than the boys who play the game? You'll go to tryouts Tuesday. You will win or lose. If you lose out this year—there's another season." He sighed. "That's life all the way, partner."

CHAPTER 5

Tryouts

ROBIN SHUDDERED when he saw the array of candidates already issued numbers. There must be two hundred, he brooded. Had there been so many the previous year? Probably so. But he hadn't hoped to qualify as a ten-year-old. He had turned in his application blank and gone through the trials because that was necessary for assignment to a minor league squad. But now—he dared to hope. So did Mark and Dave. Mark's mother had brought all three of them to the West Austin field. Rob's mother had said she might come later, even though by her own admission she would not understand anything she saw.

Robin wasn't sure he did, either. These tryouts moved so swiftly, boys were grouped and shunted from one official to another—Robin remembered his feeling of the year before, that strange men in baseball caps

ordered them here and there while the managers who
would do the actual picking showed little or no interest. He knew better now, of course. He knew that
Chase had held separate conferences with Bruce Elliott, Hugh Lance, Steve Warren and Bob Holloway.
Each had brought a list of names to the Alloway home,
their nominations for boys who deserved particular attention. Chase stood out in deep left field now, clip-
board in hand, a half dozen boys in crimson caps
crouched around him. The opinions of these boys
would influence Chase's bidding; he had said so the
previous night. At least one of these veteran players, he
explained, would know each candidate on the field, his
family, the boy's disposition, and, of course, the candidate's record in minor league play.

Rob sighed. Probably this seemed like confused
swarming to the other boys and their parents watching
anxiously from behind the fence, but a manager's stepson knew better. President Luther Thomas had visited
the Alloways briefly the previous night. When his
mother expressed doubt that four men could fairly appraise over two hundred boys in two days, the president had replied firmly. Rob recalled his exact words.

"Each manager can nominate twenty-five players for
bidding. I have marveled at it myself, Janet, but the
lists they submit will be almost identical. Every now
and then some good boy comes in as a 'sleeper' but not
often. I have gone through enough tryouts that I have
almost gotten the hang of it myself. I can prove it. I can

tell you tomorrow night which boys the managers will be fighting over."

Rob was handed a large piece of paper with the number 134 on it. Dave and Mark came right behind him. At least a dozen league officials went into action, each with his own responsibility. Mr. Thomas was at the loudspeaker.

"Your attention, please. Numbers 125 to 150 will report to the first base dugout."

Robin knew what this meant, hitting trials. The automatic pitching machine stood ready. Mr. Thomas announced other assignments. Eight groups of boys, twenty-five in each, deployed on two fields. It was hectic motion, no doubt of that. Veteran players were busy, too. Three catchers waited in full regalia. Others were catching in for the fungo hitters. Again Robin recalled Mr. Thomas's words to his mother.

"It's a great show. You will get a kick out of it, Janet."

"How will I know what is happening?"

"Watch the managers and their runners, the boys already on teams. You can tell which team they represent by their caps. Suddenly there will be one or more of them racing out to talk to one of the candidates. Then you know some boy has impressed a manager. When four runners start moving, each in a different colored cap, then you know the fight for one boy is underway, and won't be settled until the bidding is over."

The first batter took five futile swings, came to the dugout with tight lips. Robin went to the bat rack. The hitting went fast with a machine, for at least fifty balls were in use and the catchers took turns. He had used a thirty-one-inch bat in minor league, but now he settled for a thick-handled thirty. He remembered his poor showing of the year before. He had been unprepared for the machine's speed.

A full infield was set, all proven players. Hitters were supposed to swing three times, bunt twice and try to run out the last one.

Robin, satisfied with his bat, looked around him. The stands were filled with concerned parents; they also lined the fences. Robin grinned as he saw his mother sitting next to Mrs. Kelly.

Number 126 was announced as Reuben Potter. Rob knew him slightly; they had been in the same class one year. But Reuben hadn't played in the minor league. He won't do much, thought Robin.

He was wrong. Reuben slashed a hard grounder to the shortstop. He lifted two flies to left field. He missed his first bunt effort, then laid down a trickler. The third baseman was in close, but Reuben could scamper. The play at first was close. And, from separate corners of the field, came the runners just as Mr. Thomas had described them. The Giants' blue, the Cats' green, the Dodgers' maroon. No crimson cap; Rob wondered why. But three runners—Reuben Potter was in as far as his batting was concerned. Rob looked toward his mother. Could she appreciate the show now? She was talking excitedly to Mrs. Kelly. Robin grinned. He guessed that she was telling what Mr. Thomas had told her.

There was no letup. Suddenly Number 132 was at the plate. Robin now could swing his bat; only the next two batters were allowed out of the dugout. A miss, two weak dribbles, two fouled bunts and Number 133 stepped into the batters' box.

Robin took a deep breath, repeating to himself the things he must not do. He must not overswing. He must keep his back foot planted. And he must not step into the bucket under any conditions.

Number 133 reached first and was quickly intercepted by a green-capped boy. Robin moved to the plate. Mr. Thomas's announcement was the same as for the previous batters.

"Number 134, Robin Scott."

Robin was prepared for that, of course. But the ripple of applause from the stands and along the fences was something else. So was the familiar voice which drowned out the others:

"You hit that ball, Robin."

He stepped out of the box, letting the first pitch pass. No other batter had been greeted so. But no other batter had stumbled around with an old shin guard to strengthen his weak leg. And the word had spread quickly, started by Dick Flanagan. Number 134 could get a uniform simply by showing up at the tryouts. He had refused. He stood there now, bat ready, and it was no advantage to him that the crimson-capped man in left field was his stepfather.

"Just meet the ball, kid."

That was Dick Flanagan talking, crouched to receive

the pitch. It never reached him. Robin hit a ground ball to second base. He shook his head ruefully. Again he had underestimated the speed of the automatic arm. He did better on the second try, flying to center field. Then he hit a line drive to left. His first bunt effort rolled foul, but the second trickled toward first. Pitcher and first baseman hesitated; by then Robin had reached first.

He turned and a maroon-capped boy caught his arm, Gene Meador. He had glove and ball.

"Come on, Scott," he said gruffly. "Mac wants to see how you throw."

"Us next, Scott," said Paul Cannon of the Atlas Giants.

"Then us, Scott," said Wilbur Evans of the Cats, relieved that the waiting would be over.

Rob followed after Gene. It was first come, first served. There was a five-minute limit to such individual trials. Paul and Wilbur tagged right behind. Robin could not help looking toward left field. Wasn't Chase even interested? No movement from the Winston headquarters. Robin ducked his head. He supposed he had not expressed his feelings very clearly. Probably Chase had the impression that Robin did not want to play on his stepfather's team. And that was not the truth. Robin had just wanted —————

An outburst of applause made him turn. He looked too late, but he realized what had happened. Dave Presley had hit one over the left field fence! That would bring out another set of runners, Robin knew. Mark

Kelly was in the on-deck circle. "Come on, Mark," Robin whispered. Then he started throwing to Gene. Paul and Wilbur stood aside, watching closely.

"Nothing wrong with his arm," Robin heard Paul say.

Of course not, Robin thought. Nor my fielding either, which either the Cats or Atlas was sure to test next. I have had personal coaching for weeks now, stern training by the best manager on this field, better even than Jim Tracy, no matter how many titles the Giants have won. And what did I do in return? I made him believe that I did not want him to bid for me!

Robin turned again. Four boys were escorting Dave along the left field line.

"Your five minutes are up," Paul reminded Gene.

Paul had a bat and a ball. "I'll hit you a few, Scott."

It was almost like a pepper game, except that Robin fielded all the grounders himself. He stopped once. Mark had passed first base on his second bunt and Robin wanted to see what happened. Here came the charge of all four colors and Robin chortled aloud. All three of them had won special notice. But the Crimson had tagged only two!

Now Wilbur took charge of Robin. He had Robin slide, then go after two fly balls. Both were easy catches. Golly, they were right to him. He was accustomed to chasing spinning balls carefully hit just barely within his reach if he strained.

Wilbur turned to Paul and Gene, who hadn't missed a move.

"I don't see any use of trying him on anything else."

"Me either," said Paul with a shrug.

"Do you catch?" asked Gene. "I saw you wearing a shin guard.

Robin shook his head.

"Dick Flanagan told me about that," Wilbur explained. "He was just wearing it to build up a weak leg."

"Yeah, I remember."

The three veteran players looked at each other, then back at Robin.

"That's all, Scott," Gene said. "We don't have anything to do with picking the new players, but ——"

"He knows all that," interrupted Wilbur. "Don't you know who he is? Mr. Alloway's stepson."

"Oh, yeah." Gene hesitated again. "Your name just might come up at the auction, Scott. I hope so anyhow, and that we get you."

Mr. Thomas's voice came over the loudspeaker. "To simplify the tryouts and provide more playing room, the four managers have requested that the following boys leave the field." He rattled off some ten numbers, including 134, 135 and 136. Then he added, "The league officials have no voice in the selection of players, so I say this at my own risk in order to reassure partially the parents of the boys being dismissed so early. My guess is that the managers have already decided to bid on these players at tomorrow night's auction."

A ripple of applause started as the ten designated players were directed to the players' agent's table to surrender their numbers; it mounted as the happy young group darted for the water fountain.

Mark hugged Robin. "All three of us!" he gloated. "Mr. Alloway did it, too."

Robin nodded, not trusting himself to speak. Chase had helped Mark and Dave, sure, but they might have earned uniforms without him. What about a boy who was awkward because he favored one leg and so couldn't run or move out of his tracks to catch a ball!

"My mother is here," Robin told Mark, "so I'll ride home with her. She might want to go right now."

He was wrong again. His mother hugged and kissed him right there in the stands—despite his struggles—but refused to leave. She was enjoying it, she said. She would enjoy the rest of the tryout even more, now that she wasn't worried about her son.

"I almost fainted when I saw those three boys charging down on you," she told him with a laugh. "If I hadn't talked to Mr. Thomas last night, I wouldn't have known what it meant."

"Me either," Robin admitted. "I guess I didn't pay attention to things like that last year."

He was tempted to say something about the Crimson's indifference to his showing, then caught himself in time. It had been his idea. He had asked his mother to talk to Chase in his behalf. His lips twitched. Him and his fool pride. Why hadn't he been willing to be an option player!

CHAPTER 6

A Crimson Cap

Robin, Mark and Dave watched the second day of tryouts from the stands. These aspirants were the younger boys, eight, nine and ten. It wasn't nearly as exciting as the previous day's activity. Several boys, most of them ten years old, showed promise. No more than ten would be selected, and the others would be assigned to teams in the minor league or the "peewee" league, limited to eight- and nine-year-olds.

Baseball for every boy—the West Austin League guaranteed it. But the real thrill was to be on a major league team. Robin had tossed and squirmed most of the previous night, too excited to sleep. Mark and Dave confessed to the same feeling. Others of the outstanding ten joined them until they sat in a solid group, bound together by great common experience. There was tall twelve-year-old Joe Carlson. He would dominate the auction; Robin was sure of that. Will Davis, Eddie McNew, Dave Reagan, Charlie Hagan—Robin had played with them and against them in the minor league. They, like Mark and Dave, had grown in a year's time. Had improved, too.

Most had team preferences, but voiced them discreetly. *Any* team would do. The majority hoped for an Atlas uniform, to play under Jim Tracy, the perennial winner, who had coached an all-star team to the finals at Williamsport. Robin eagerly drank in all information about the returning players of each team. The emphasis was on pitchers, of course. Atlas had Ramon Alvarez and Joe Pittman back. The Dodgers were well fixed with Bill Roberts and Curt Cooley. But, said Dick Flanagan, the Crimson combination of Bruce Elliott and Lefty Lance matched any pair in the league. The Reds would have won last year if Mr. Alloway had had even one outstanding hitter. The Calumet Cats boasted only one experienced hurler, Wilbur Evans. But Manager Kane had a surplus of points from previous seasons. He could get Carlson, said Dick. And Carlson could pitch with any boy in the league, declared the Maroon catcher.

Robin stored each fact in his mind. For he was part of this now. Chase had confirmed Mr. Thomas's prediction the night before. Certainly no one would send ten boys off in humiliation. The coaches simply wanted them out of the way to concentrate on other prospects.

"Aren't you proud of Robin?" Mrs. Alloway had asked.

Chase had smiled. "Not especially. He didn't look any better than I expected him to."

He had been silent a moment, then added, "But I did appreciate the applause for him." He turned to his stepson. "That made up for all the teasing and tormenting, didn't it?"

Robin agreed, and withheld any mention of the Crimson's failure to send out a scout.

Dick Flanagan was talking about Chase now; Robin put aside thoughts of the previous evening.

"He's the only manager who has never won a pennant, but he's a good one anyhow. I sure like him."

"Is he as hard on his boys as Mac Collins is?"

"Golly, no. But Mac lets us have a lot of fun. He starts it himself sometimes. The spectators never see that side of him."

Robin's thoughts drifted off again. So Chase was the only coach who hadn't stepped into the winner's spot! Robin's lip trembled. That wasn't right. But he could not even hope for his stepfather to win this season. He would be on an opposing team, him and his big mouth.

Mr. Thomas's voice signaled the end of the tryouts. The auction would start at eight o'clock, but no players would be informed of their selection until morning.

Chase came over to make sure Rob had a ride home. He did; Mrs. Presley was coming for them.

"Good. Tell your mother not to wait up for me. We are having dinner with the president and the players' agent, then we'll start bidding. And these things go on for hours. We haven't finished once before two o'clock."

Robin delivered the message. His mother shook her head.

"I *shall* wait up for him. I am not going to sleep until I find out what team you are on." She smiled. "Chase is going to tease the life out of me this summer. I kept insisting that I would not be involved in baseball, but one day—that one time you came to bat—I couldn't even breathe, Robin." She shook her blonde head. "I don't see how I can possibly survive this summer, but I don't intend to miss a single game."

Robin's lip trembled. "I wish I hadn't—well, Mom, I would *like* to play for Chase's team. I just didn't want ——"

"I understand," she said gently. She hugged him. "He does, too, honey. A man just can't walk into your life and become your father. But he has been considerate of you since that first day. Stern about some things, like your leg." Tears welled in her eyes. "He made up in weeks for what I had failed to do in two years."

"He sure did," Robin sighed. He choked back a sob. "I wish I had let him take me as an option player."

"Then you wouldn't have won the respect you have now. I've had many people tell me how they admire your courage and attitude. Mr. Thomas did. He said he hoped this established a precedent."

Robin shook his head. "I don't care. I would have been on Chase's team."

She patted his cheek. "It's too late now, honey. Crying about it won't help."

"I know it." He heaved a deep sigh. "Well, I'll find

out tomorrow who I play for." His lips went tight. "And whichever team it is, I'll do my best every time we play Chase's bunch."

"That's exactly what Chase wants you to do."

The doorbell awoke Robin early next morning. Ordinarily he would have only turned over and gone right back to sleep, but he recognized Mark's voice.

"Is Mr. Alloway up yet, Mrs. Alloway?"

"Barely," his mother answered. "I'll call him."

Robin ran to the open window. Mark and Dave stood on the porch.

"You don't have to bother him, Mrs. Alloway," Mark said. "We just want him to know—well, Dave and I wouldn't have made a team without him. We appreciate it and ——"

"He enjoys being bothered by such matters. Here he is now."

Robin hurried down the steps, not bothering to put on a bathrobe. Chase, still in his dressing gown, stood talking to the boys.

"I wanted both of you," he was saying, "but the bidding got too steep for me. You made quite an impression in tryouts."

"Your help did it, Mr. Alloway," Dave said. "You taught us more in a day than we learned all last year. It's not going to be easy to play against you."

"You'll get over that in a day," Chase said lightly. "Congratulations, boys, and thanks for coming by."

Robin had restrained himself long enough. "What about me?" he demanded.

"That can wait a minute," Chase said maddeningly. He shook hands with both Dave and Mark. "Have a good season."

"Yes, sir. Good-by, Mr. Alloway."

Chase closed the door and faced his stepson. "Mark went to Atlas and Dave to Calumet."

"And me?"

"You cost some points," Chase sighed. "Mac Collins was especially strong for you."

"But ——"

His mother intervened. She put her arms around Robin's shoulder.

"Chase never had any intention of letting you go to another team."

Robin trembled. "Why didn't you tell me that last night, Mom?"

"I wasn't sure. He hadn't told me and I didn't want to ask him." Her lips formed a smile, but her eyes moistened. "I couldn't ask him to take you, honey, any more than you could." She hugged him tighter. "I'm not used to it either—having a man in the house to depend on."

"If that man doesn't get some breakfast soon," Chase said gruffly, "he just might spank both of you."

Chase told them a little about the auction. Each team was allotted ten thousand points to bid for players. Any points not used one year carried over to the next. Sneaker Kane of the Cats had six thousand points so accumulated.

"We knew he would get Joe Carlson. We made him pay nine thousand points."

"For one player!" Mrs. Alloway exclaimed.

"Sure. That boy can chunk. He's the difference between Sneaker having a ball club or not. Then we were after Will Davis. Jim Tracy had to buy a catcher."

Robin interrupted. He didn't remember Will.

"Good glove boy," said Chase. "Jim had him off with both Alvarez and Pittman pitching to him. The rest of us let him alone but our boys were scouting him. Steve thinks he might be the best catcher in the league. I believe we fooled Jim for once. We sure tried to, anyhow. We took turns bidding for him."

"The spectators should know how these things work beforehand," said his wife. "The parents sit there in the stands and wonder at all the commotion. They have no idea that you managers are planning so carefully."

"I guess not," Chase admitted with a grin. "That's baseball—fans thinking they can run the team better than the managers can." He sighed. "It was Mac and me then. He is hard to outfigure. You have to run up the price—make the other managers spend their points so you can get the boys you want. Mac needs glove men; I was after hitters."

Robin recalled Dick Flanagan's analysis of last year's Crimson team—probably a pennant winner if blessed with even one strong batter.

"Who did we get?" he asked. He could wait no longer.

"Eddie McNew, Dave Reagan and you."

"We got Eddie! He hit over five hundred in the minor league."

"I know. Then Wright Hartung and Jim Holloway, of course, on option."

"Are you satisfied, dear?"

"Very," Chase said. "I had a starting defensive lineup already, all but one outfielder. But they are glove boys. I will have platoon this year; we'll send in more pinch hitters than this league ever saw." He sighed and gestured for his coffee cup to be refilled. "We have never won a title. We were second last year; the Giants had a little better team. We had no bench at all. This year we do."

"What do you mean by bench?"

"Substitutes and replacements. Boys get sick or hurt, close relatives die, and, like adults, they have days when they can't do a thing right. That is the real edge Jim Tracy has held on this league for five straight seasons. We are at least even with him this year in that respect. Now if I can just match him in strategy!"

"You can do that, I know."

"Do you know Tracy?"

"I've met him."

"Nobody beats him in any game without bleeding. Sneaker Kane and Mac Collins are just as tough." Chase shook his head. "All three have coached rings around me and I'm the first to admit it. But this year—" his eyes shone— "unless I'm dead wrong, we have the boys."

"This bench—your plans put Robin in that group?"

"Oh, yes. I think his natural position is first base.

Bruce Elliott and Lefty Lance alternate between there and the mound."

"Eddie McNew can pitch," Robin said, concealing his disappointment well. He had hoped for more than this certain role of a substitute.

"I know it. He will work some this season, too. He can play infield, too. He may take over at second base."

Robin excused himself and went outside. Sitting on the front steps, he struggled with his disappointment. A long season was ahead of him; he did not like sitting in the dugout. His lips went tight. He might just crowd one of his stepfather's defensive stars out of the lineup. Nobody had expected him to be a standout in the trials either.

But that determination was shaken the very next day. The Reds held their first practice. Chase stationed his veterans at their regular positions. Robin saw that his stepfather had trained each one as patiently and carefully as he had worked with Robin, Mark and Dave. The infielders flipped the ball around smoothly, showing the results of many "pepper" sessions. The outfielders could back up against the fence to pull down fly balls. And Robin saw that Mr. Elliott, Bruce's father, used a fungo bat as well as Chase; that meant never hitting the ball directly to a fielder.

Robin could not deny, either, that Eddie McNew seemed to be the best of the new players.

Then came his turn in the field—his, Dave's, and the other new players'. Rob had brought his first baseman's mitt and he ran happily to take that position. Yes, *ran*—with a speed which surprised him.

Chase hit easier chances to these new additions. Still they fumbled and threw wild to first base. The first throw could not be reached by any boy of Rob's stature, but he drew the manager's criticism along with the shortstop.

"You couldn't reach the throw, Rob, but you could have kept it from going to the fence. It's giving the other side an extra base to just stand on the bag and stab at empty air. Move to stop the overthrow, and I mean *move*."

"Yes, sir," Rob muttered, pounding the pocket of his mitt.

Shortly Mr. Elliott called him to task, too.

"You're using that mitt like a glove, Scott," the assistant manager said sharply. "It isn't one, not at all. You wear it loose. I'll show you."

Rob watched carefully. "You don't catch the ball, you snatch it. Between the laces, not in the pocket like a glove." Mr. Elliott returned the mitt. "These boys aren't pegging bullets. You will see what I mean when you work out with Bob and Dick. You take their pegs in the palm of your hand and you'll have bruised flesh."

"Yes, sir," Rob promised.

He tried to follow instructions and let the first throw trickle out of his mitt. He looked helplessly to Mr. Elliott.

"You will get the hang of it," the assistant manager said encouragingly. "You should have seen Bruce two years ago. He went crying to his mother that I was ruining him as a fielder."

He wouldn't do that, Robin whispered. But he was not sure at all that he would ever master the so-called snatch. It seemed awkward to him.

Then, as Mr. Alloway called in the new players to bat and the veterans to field, Rob observed how Lefty Lance grabbed pegs. The twelve-year-old seemed to snare the ball between thumb and first finger. And there surely was no doubt that a throw from Bob Holloway or Dick Mattingly would sting any boy's palm.

Roger Pearson was throwing batting practice. The Crimson manager had ordered two-thirds speed, but Rob was sure that the pitches came harder than that. To him, at least. He missed three straight swings, then sent an easy roller toward first base. He sighed in disgust as he returned the bat to the rack outside the dugout. Neither manager ordered him anywhere and Rob leaned against the dugout and watched Dave Reagan cut.

Dave sent the first pitch whistling over second base, lifted a fly, hit a difficult grounder which Bob Holloway fielded expertly.

Roger must have stopped throwing at full speed, decided Rob, else Dave would not have connected so solidly. Dave had been a steady hitter in minor league competition but no better than Rob. Nor had he been better in workouts, either.

Robin heaved a deep sigh. Maybe he was trying too hard—pressing, as the boys said.

He mentioned that shyly to his stepfather on the way home.

"I thought so," Chase said easily. "You seemed to be tight, all tied up in knots. But don't worry about first-day jitters. I had them myself."

"Dave Reagan didn't act nervous."

"No," the manager agreed. "He seems to be the calm sort, a good competitor. He impressed me that way in tryouts."

Robin's mother came out to meet them as Chase stopped the station wagon in the driveway.

"How was practice?"

"The first day," the manager replied with a shrug. "You can't tell one way or the other."

"How did you do?"

Robin hesitated at the direct question. "Not good," he said unhappily. "I guess I was nervous."

"How did your leg hold out?"

Robin grinned sheepishly. It hurt a little, now that he thought about it. But it hadn't bothered him in practice, he said. Chase, however, stated otherwise.

"He still favors it," the manager said. "He doesn't react as he should. But he is certainly improving."

CHAPTER 7

Business Looks Up

IMPROVING MAYBE, but not enough. Robin realized that anew in the second practice. The two managers divided responsibility for defensive drills, Chase working the infield, Mr. Elliott putting the outfielders through their paces. And apparently all those not considered as regular infielders were grouped automatically as fly chasers.

Robin disliked outfield play; he was a poor judge of fly balls and knew it. Mr. Carowe had experimented with him briefly in the outfield, then had settled him at first base. That, he was convinced, was his natural position. But with Hugh Lance and Bruce Elliott alternating between pitcher's mound and the first sack—what chance did Robin have of playing at his favorite spot?

What hope, either, for outfield duty? Dave Reagan looked better than Robin, though Dave's experience was all in the infield. A ten-year-old newcomer, Wright Hartung, caught flies better than either of them. But Wright, a slight and nervous youngster, showed little at the plate.

Chase devoted most of that second drill to hitting practice, especially bunting. Robin had considered himself almost an expert at laying the ball down, but the stance taught him by Mr. Carowe did not suit the Crimson manager.

"I know what you have been taught," Chase told his squad. "You have learned to square around in the box. You haven't tried to keep the other team from knowing you intend to lay the ball down. That is the usual Little League style. But we are going to learn to bunt like big leaguers. No shifting of the feet, just meeting the ball."

He showed what he meant. Robin nodded. So Pee-wee Reese demonstrated bunting in commercials on the "Game of the Week" telecasts.

"This is something new for all of you," said Chase. "And don't think we won't use the bunt a lot this season. You new boys are starting even with Bob, Lefty and everybody else. You can get into the lineup on your bunting alone. For we intend to use our bench this season. I won't hesitate a minute to send in a pinch hitter."

The tall manager and Mr. Elliott took turns throwing batting practice. Five swings, three bunt efforts—the workout was nearly over before Mr. Alloway started the regular defensive drill.

Eddie McNew was the only new player assigned a position.

"But I want you others to watch every move and listen to every word," Chase told the other six Reds. "There is a certain place to go every time the ball is hit."

Most of his veterans remembered their assignments. Robin watched enviously as Hugh and Bruce divided time at first base. Especially was he impressed by their catlike pounces on bunts and their quick throws. Eddie was troubled by his responsibility to cover the bag on such plays. He must take the peg inside the baseline, insisted Chase, usually before touching the base.

"Try crossing the bag," warned the manager, "and some runner will knock you loose from the ball. The baseline belongs to the runner; never forget that."

The right fielder was supposed to back up such throws.

Robin, Dave, Sam and Wright took over the outfield positions. Mr. Elliott moved from one to the other, schooling them to change positions according to the play's direction. Robin was in left field. A hit to the right side of the diamond—his move was to protect any overthrow of second on a single, to back up third if the hit was for extra bases.

Chase's voice rose loud and impatient when any boy failed to move, or started late.

"Take off with the crack of the bat," he said over and over.

Another disappointing showing, Robin mused on the way home. He sighed. Golly, there was so much to be learned. His left leg ached, too; he was conscious of that even before his mother's concerned question. The last two laps around the field had done it, he decided. And, according to boys experienced in the league, Chase was the "easiest" of the four managers! Robin groaned. What must it be like to play for Mac Collins?

The next day was worse. Chase took the bat himself and assigned the six substitutes as base-runners. Safeties did not count against the defense, only errors and stolen bases. If such an unearned run scored, then around the field for the regulars, on the double.

The drill was harder on the runners than the fielders; as Dave, Sam and the others agreed. Chase hit almost every pitch; each time a runner sprinted for first.

Batting practice finally, but no letup for the six newcomers. Mr. Elliott lofted fly balls to them while the regulars took their five cut and three bunts.

More infield, as Robin, Dave and the others came in to hit, Chase batting ground balls from behind first base. Bruce was throwing, but Robin found his offerings easier to hit than Roger's pitches. Robin connected squarely with the second throw, slashing a line drive down the left field foul line.

"That's getting good wood," called out Mr. Elliott.

Robin could not help beaming. His first praise since the start of practice!

His bunts now. His first effort rolled foul, but his second try trickled to a stop halfway between the plate and third base. His last poke was fair, too, toward first.

"That's the way to lay the ball down," approved Mr. Elliott. "See that, you twelve-year-old knuckleheads? If

Scott can learn it in three days, what's wrong with you?"

"We're just used to the other style, Mr. Elliott," Bob Holloway said apologetically.

"Then get unused to it," ordered the assistant manager. "We can't win without runs. And it looks like we'll have to bunt to move runners around."

The usual two laps—it seemed as if each step would be Robin's last. But he staggered in ahead of several teammates, including catcher Steve Warren.

Tomorrow at the same time, directed Chase.

"When are we going to play a practice game, Mr. Alloway?"

The question came from Hugh Lance. The manager hesitated.

"We still need more hitting, Lefty," he said finally. "And I'm not ready for you and Bruce to start bearing down."

"The Dodgers and the Cats played today," Bob said.

"Sure," nodded the Crimson manager. "They are farther along than we are."

"But we have the same lineup back, almost," Bruce persisted. "Let Roger pitch if you are worried about Lefty or me hurting our arms."

"We won't play until next week," Chase said firmly, "and then we'll use the new boys half the time."

Robin's face brightened. That meant he would get to play then.

He replaced Lefty at first base in the third inning.

The Giants led 5-3 by then; Roger had showed poor control in the first two innings. Lefty took the mound and fanned three out of four batters. Bruce had sat on the sidelines until now; he took first and Robin went to left field.

He came to bat with Dave on first and none out. His stepfather's signal came as a surprise; Robin had expected the bunt sign. But hitting away was even better, of course; he met the second pitch squarely and sent a ground ball between short and third.

His first hit! In his first time up, too. He readjusted his helmet and called hopefully to Wright Hartung. No bunt sign from the bench—Robin shook his head. What better situation than this for a sacrifice? Two runs behind, a weak swinger up, none out. Bob Holloway crouched in the on-deck circle.

But hit away—the Crimson coach made no effort to conceal his signal. Wright struck out, Bob fouled to the catcher, Luke Callahan rolled weakly to first base.

So the game ended—5-3. Two laps—Robin plodded along behind Maury and Stuart. Why such emphasis on bunts in practice if they were not to move up runners in an actual game?

He could not resist asking that question on the way home.

"We will hit away in all practice games," Chase said casually. "We need all the hitting practice we can get."

Robin licked his dry lips. "I had one for two," he said shyly.

"So did Dave," pointed out the manager. "Both of

you are coming along at the plate. Young Hartung can field, but he hasn't touched a ball with a bat. He steps into the bucket, too."

Robin waited for his stepfather's comments about the other three new players, but Chase did not mention them.

"The Giants didn't look so good," Robin suggested.

"Not today." A smile touched the tall man's features. "Jim Tracy will have his troubles this year, even more than we will."

Robin frowned. Still, the Giants had won, even with Mr. Tracy using four pitchers. If Atlas was so weak but could still defeat Winston, then where did that put the Crimson? In the cellar? Robin sighed. He just could not believe the other teams were that strong.

Hitting, hitting, hitting—three days of it, almost solid—two-thirds of each practice devoted to it. Five swings, three bunts, then around again, with Chase watching each batter closely, suggesting changed stances or raised shoulders.

Then, most days, a sort of workup—six boys in bat until put out, then another set of hitters. This type of practice pleased Robin most, for he and Dave Reagan improved at the plate, in bunting as well as hitting away.

Fielding drills were short and hurried, concentration on the veteran players, brief outfield stints for Robin, Dave and the other rookies.

On the mound through these batting sessions—gosh, who *didn't* take a pitching turn? Lefty, Bruce and Roger each afternoon, Mr. Elliott until his arm tired, sometimes Chase, Dick and Bob. None of the boys threw curves, but the two coaches offered every sort of tantalizer.

Neither Lefty nor Bruce, said Chase on the way home, would try curves until a week before the opening game.

Robin remembered the repeated warnings of Dizzy Dean to all young ball players. Did it really hurt a boy's arm to throw curves?

"Not if he knows how to throw one and doesn't overdo it," Chase said. "I know where you heard that. But if curves are so hard on the arm, why is it that the older pitchers turn to the breaking stuff—sliders, knucklers and so on? I can throw a knuckler about as well as I ever could."

"I wouldn't want to pitch," mused Robin.

He saw his stepfather's lips tighten. "You don't want to play the outfield either, do you?"

"No, sir," Robin said before he thought. Then he added hurriedly, "I just don't have the knack for judging fly balls."

"One simple thing would help you. Don't start in for the fly until you are sure. Nothing is sillier than a boy starting to charge in and then having to double back. He misses that kind nearly every time."

Robin sighed. He was guilty of that often.

When was the next practice game? He was as

impatient as his teammates. The Dodgers and Calumet had played four games, the Giants three.

"We will try the Cats Friday," Chase said.

"Are we out to beat them or will we take turns playing?"

The manager smiled at Bob's question. "We will try to beat them," he said mildly. "I don't recall ever losing to anyone intentionally."

"Then Lefty or Bruce will pitch?"

"Two innings each," Chase said calmly. "Roger will finish up."

"What about the regular lineup? Can we stay in four or five innings anyhow?"

"I was not aware that we *had* a regular lineup as yet," Mr. Alloway said carefully. "Or have *you* settled on one?"

"Gosh, no," Bob said quickly. "But I thought maybe the boys back from last year ——"

"If you can hold your positions. What about hitting? It seems to me that Dave and Rob are showing up some of you veterans at the plate."

With that the manager turned and walked away, leaving mixed feelings among the boys behind him. At least two were pleased and did not try to hide it. Rob felt like jumping up and down. He had been daring to speculate on his chances of earning a starting position. He had been sure that he was outhitting some of the veterans, the outfielders especially. But it was great to hear the manager say so!

He started against Calumet, and Dave, too. Chase

read the batting order quite casually—Scott in left field, Reagan in right. Sixth and seventh in the batting order.

Joe Carlson started for the Cats. The twelve-year-old rookie threw hard but showed poor control. He walked Bob, Lefty and Bruce while fanning Bruce and Eddie. That brought up Robin in a clutch situation indeed, two away and ducks on the pond.

He wiped his hands on the resin bag and set his feet firmly. He had read somewhere that runs batted in—RBI's—impressed a manager more than any other statistic. A base knock now might well mean another chance in the starting lineup.

He backed away from the first pitch. It had whistled much too close to his head for comfort. He took a deep breath and rubbed his hands in the dirt again. It would not be easy to stand in against Carlson or to keep from swinging at wild pitches. But the batter who could get wood against such chunking was sure to record many base hits.

Another ball, low and outside. Two-nothing. Robin looked to his stepfather. Take? The same signal came, hit away. Robin choked up on his bat and stood even closer to the plate. This throw came in high and hard. Robin swung. His blood surged wildly as he started for first base. He had connected and no doubt of it.

But his solid smash went straight to right fielder Jim Dunlap. A long out, groaned Robin, but still an out. The Reds retired without a run.

Lineup changes—Rob and Dave to the bench—Sam, Wright and Jim into the lineup, Roger to the mound, then Eddie. For the Calumet bats exploded and the Crimson batters failed to produce a single run. Final score—Cats 7, Reds 0.

Robin held back the question he wanted to ask on the way home. Shouldn't his stepfather be concerned about this one-sided defeat? If so, Chase gave only one indication.

"Starting tomorrow," he said casually, "you and Dave will work more in the outfield."

CHAPTER 8

Oh, What a Glorious Day!

THE DODGERS impressed Robin as the strongest team in the league. Mac Collins' starters hit Bruce regularly for two innings, and the Winston infield seemed to do everything wrong. Lefty squelched the Bedford hitters in his two-inning turn, but the score stood 6-1 at the end of the fourth.

These scores had come against the regulars, brooded Robin; the Giants and the Cats had gotten their early leads against a lineup spotted with new players. The first two practice games could be shrugged off as unimportant, but what about this reversal? Both Curt Cooley and Gene Meador had outpitched their Crimson rivals.

Chase was displeased with his regulars; he said so after the fourth inning.

"I thought you were ready to play a ball game," he

said sternly. "But I see you aren't. We will try the new players then. They can't do any worse."

Three of them did better—Robin, Dave and Wright, especially at the plate. Of course they faced relief hurlers—Ralph Fenton and Bill Galloway—Robin reminded Dave of that as they swapped compliments after the game. Each had smashed drives to the wall for extra bases. Wright had beaten out a slow roller and made a fine catch in center field. Both Robin and Dave had crossed the plate, too, making the final score 6-3.

Robin had caught his only chance in left field, too, an easy fly right in his hands. Maybe Chase would start him in the next and last practice game, against the Giants. According to the talk of other boys, the other three starting lineups were settled already. Neither Dave nor Mark expected to be regulars; in fact, neither had played as much in practice games as Robin.

"Every time I'm watching," Mark said disgustedly, "you are out in left field. I sure never thought you would make any starting lineup this year."

"I am hitting pretty good," Robin said, and he couldn't help the proud note in his voice.

"Sure," grunted Mark, "against relief pitchers." He hesitated, then said disgustedly, "Maybe it helps to be on your stepfather's team."

Robin flared up. "That isn't so and you know it."

"I don't know whether it is or not," Mark snapped. "Mr. Alloway has boys back for every position. I know that. And he bought a fine player in Eddie McNew. What business do you have starting on a team like that?"

Dave came to Robin's aid. "Aw, you're just sore because you're not playing more," he told Mark. "Sure Mr. Alloway has a bunch of regulars from last year. But look where they finished—fourth. And look at this year—Winston hasn't won a game. It's just an easier lineup to break into, that's all. Rob is hitting good. He slammed one hard off Joe Carlson."

"That makes sense," Mark admitted. "Winston is sure the fourth place team."

"Oh, go jump in the lake," Robin said angrily.

"You want to make me?" Mark challenged.

They had been sitting on Robin's curb, but now all three were on their feet, Dave pushing between Mark and Robin.

"Cut out the squabbling," Dave ordered, speaking to both but looking at Mark. "You ought to be glad Rob is getting to play. I just wish I was."

"I am," Mark said at once. "I hope he gets to play all the time."

He left with that, Dave at his heels. Robin looked after them glumly a minute, then went into the house. His mother noticed his unhappy expression almost at once. What was the trouble?

"Nothing much. Mark and I just had some words."

"What in the world about?"

"He made me mad."

"I can see that for myself," his mother said with a smile. "But what about?"

"He said I was getting to play because—well, Chase was *letting* me—because ———"

"Do you believe that?"

Robin looked at her a moment before answering. "I sure don't," he said finally. "He is my stepfather, but I am getting better all the time."

"Chase thinks so," Mrs. Alloway said gently. "He told me so last night. He thinks you will get to play some this year."

Robin's face fell. "Just *some*?"

"Won't that satisfy you? A month ago you just wanted to be on a team, any team."

"But we're losing. We've lost every game. And I'm hitting better than some of his starters."

"How about your fielding? And your leg?"

Robin could not help smiling. He had not even thought about his leg in several days. "It doesn't bother me any more," he said.

"Then you've already gotten enough from this season to make it worth while," declared his mother. "I'm certainly happy over your development. And Chase is pleased, too. Nor would I worry about his showing you any partiality. He is too good a manager for that and you know it."

"Sure," nodded Robin. He hesitated again, then sighed; he could not help it. "But I think we ought to be winning some of our games. It just isn't right for us to lose every time."

"I would be worried, too, if I knew anything about the game," Mrs. Alloway said. "As it is, I have no choice but to trust the manager. And Chase appears to be satisfied."

"He is!"

"He certainly is. In fact, he told me last night that the Reds have the best chance of winning this year that they ever had."

"If he thinks that," Robin said slowly, "then I guess I'm in the same boat with you."

When Chase drove up, the Winston Reds immediately halted their workup game and hurried to the dugout. The quartet of Sam Goldstein, Wright Hartung, Jim Holloway and Luther Callahan hurried to open the trunk. The nine- and ten-year-olds had that responsibility, as well as keeping up with the bats and balls.

It was an ordinary practice, except that it was shorter than usual, ending when Mr. Thomas drove up. The league president parked just behind the dugout and started taking boxes out of his car.

"I'll send you some help, Luke," Chase called, gesturing that practice was over.

Steve Warren was first to guess the reason for this interruption.

"Uniforms!" he yelled.

Immediately Mr. Thomas had a swarm of eager helpers.

"Come on, come on," chided Chase. "This isn't a rat race. Line up."

"I want number 7 again," requested Lefty Lance.

"All right. All twelve-year-olds get the same numbers they had last year."

"Will they fit that way, Chase?" asked Mr. Thomas.

"I ordered them so they would."

"Brand new!" gasped Lefty as he ripped open his box.

"All new uniforms this year," the president said proudly.

Robin drew number 12. He could have danced with glee after stroking the cream-colored shirt and trousers, with crimson trim, and the crimson socks. Then came the caps, crimson with a cream W.

"You can start wearing the caps right now," said Chase. "They belong to you. The uniforms you turn back at the end of the season, of course, but not the caps." His blue eyes twinkled. "And you young knuckleheads respect an old man's prejudice. They are *not* hats."

Robin's fitted perfectly.

"Try the suits on when you get home. No alterations without asking me first. The pants are baggy. They will stay baggy. I want you to look like ball players, anyhow, and ball players don't wear tight-fitting breeches."

"Oh, gosh, Mr. Alloway." The groan came from Dick Mattingly. Others echoed it.

"I mean that, Dick, and you know it. Now these are *your* uniforms. You earned them yourselves. I want you to keep up with them *yourselves*. Don't expect your mother to do it. That's all today. Same time tomorrow."

Robin plopped into the front seat, still admiring the cotton garments. His stepfather smiled as he started the motor.

"They *are* nice," he conceded.

"I can't wait to show it to Mother."

Chase smiled. "She won't like it at first."

"Why not?"

"It will make you look bigger—and older."

"I guess it will," Robin sighed. "We got only T-shirts in the minor league."

"I know," Chase answered. "There's a difference, and you pay the price for it. You do for everything. In the minor league every boy gets to play in every game. Not in this league."

Robin's face clouded. "I won't get to play much, will I?"

"Only spot playing unless somebody is out," Chase said casually. "You and Dave will help us. Wright Hartung, too."

"A ten-year-old?"

"He can field and throw."

They were home by then, and Robin hurried in with his new treasures. His mother was as delighted as he was until he stood before her in full regalia. Then her smile faded.

"Why, he looks . . . he looks fourteen or fifteen."

Robin grinned at his stepfather. "What's so funny?" asked his mother.

"Chase told me you'd say that."

"Mr. Alloway is all-wise and all-knowing," she retorted. "It might be a good idea to record all remarks made about him behind the screen. It just might deflate his ego."

"A manager who has never won a pennant hasn't

much ego left," Chase said ruefully. "But this is a new year. I'll remind the knuckleheads of that tomorrow. Winston has never lost a game in these uniforms." He rubbed his chin. "Nor have we ever won an opening game. We will know Saturday if the new uniforms have broken our jinx."

"You play the Dodgers, don't you?"

Chase nodded to his wife's question. "The second best in the league, right now."

"Which team is the best?"

His eyes twinkled. "We are."

"Without winning a practice game?"

"We play the Giants again Wednesday," he said. "You'll see the difference."

And difference there was indeed. Lefty Lance started and blanked the Giants for three innings. But Hugh had hurled well every time; the change was in the Crimson offensive strategy. Winston scored in the first inning. Bob caught the Giants by surprise with his bunt; since the batter had not squared around, the Atlas infield had kept to the regular deep positions. Bob went to second on a passed ball and came home on Lefty's single.

Another Crimson tally in the third—a walk, two bunts, and Stuart crossed the plate.

Two-nothing after three full frames. Bruce took over the mound and retired the side in order. Golly, gloated Robin, we are going to win a game. And he got to play; Chase put both him and Dave into the lineup. Robin replaced Lefty at first base, Dave went to right field.

The Giants scored in the fifth; Robin and Dave singled after a walk to Steve to make the score 3-1.

Then, in the sixth, Chase put all four other new players into the game. An error by Sam Goldstein, a wild throw by Jim Holloway, two passed balls by Luke Callahan, and the Giants pulled ahead 4-3.

So the game ended, but Chase had only encouraging words.

"Don't worry about that last inning," he said, sitting on the dugout steps. "We had a lead and we could have held it. I know that as well as you do. But this was the last chance to let every boy play. The important thing is that we know what we can do as a team and the boys who can do it for us. We still made some mistakes. We will work on those Thursday and Friday. And maybe we can surprise some people Saturday."

"We'll eat 'em up," vowed Bruce. "This is *our* year!"

CHAPTER 9

Down with the Jinx!

ROBIN AWOKE EARLY, at least an hour before his stepfather. This was it, opening day! A perfect day, too; the
sunlight streamed through his window, blue jays
squawked happily on their oaken perches. The only
wrong thing he could think of was this afternoon's
schedule; Calumet and Atlas played the first game of
the usual doubleheader. That contest was scheduled to
start at 2 P.M. It might be four o'clock before the Reds
took the field, and Robin wasn't sure he could wait that
long. Why couldn't they have played this morning?
How could he pass the time between now and 1:30
when Chase had told them to report?

His new uniform was draped over a chair by his bed.
Robin wanted to put it on then and there, but knew
better; Chase would not allow him to wear it all morning even if his mother consented. Why weren't they up

and stirring about? It was Saturday, all right, but not the usual Saturday.

Then he heard his stepfather descending the steps and followed suit. Chase took coffee and newspaper to the screened porch; Robin followed with a glass of orange juice.

"Nine Little Leagues opening today," said his stepfather. "I can remember when there were just two."

"Was ours the first in Austin?"

"The third. It wasn't much of a league then, either. No grandstand, no grass on the infield, volunteer umpires—you kids have it good."

"We sure do," agreed Robin, thinking of his new uniform. He hesitated, then ventured, "Who will start— Lefty?"

"No baseball talk until game time," Chase said firmly. He pushed to his feet. "But we can have breakfast. How do you want your eggs?"

Robin sighed. His breakfast menu had changed, too, since his mother's marriage. Chase Alloway believed in eggs, meat, fruit and milk each morning. Breakfast, he insisted, was the most important meal of the day. Scrambled eggs, sausage—he cleaned his plate. Chase left for a business appointment; Mrs. Alloway leisurely scanned the newspaper as she ate. Robin sighed. How could they be so calm?

The hours finally dragged by; Robin wolfed a cold beef sandwich, then put on his uniform. How did he look? His mother sort of gurgled. Just wonderful, she said.

He decided to go on to the field, though it was just one o'clock. A group in crimson caps had gathered in the third-base bleachers; Robin joined them. Calumet was holding batting practice.

"Will we get to hit any?" worried Eddie.

"Sure," said Lefty. "We'll stay here for the ceremony, then hustle to the minor league diamond. We'll bat an hour anyhow."

Chase and Mr. Elliott arrived and gathered the Reds around the third base gate. Robin watched Mr. Thomas and other officials set up a field microphone. Little Richard Pryor, the television personality, would serve as master of ceremonies. His program had been Robin's favorite once, but he had outgrown this childish taste, now preferring Uncle Jay.

But still it was impressive business, especially as the four teams formed as many lines on the field and each boy was introduced. Little Richard told a joke or two; Robin joined in the polite applause. The flag went up slowly in center field; the "Star-Spangled Banner" was played—the usual scratchy record, too—and the red-capped boys hurried to waiting automobiles.

Three cuts, two bunts—around again—back to Knebel Field. The first game was already in the fifth inning, with Calumet leading 4-2.

Both grandstands were filled now; Robin's eyes searched the rows of faces until he saw his mother.

"Mom's here," he whispered to his stepfather.

"I expected her," was the quiet answer. "She is getting to like baseball just a little."

The last out, the triumphant shouting and dancing of the victorious Cats, the dugouts quickly emptied, and refilled with new young faces.

"The second game," Robin heard, "will start in approximately fifteen minutes."

Seven minutes of defensive drill each. Both Bruce and Lefty went to warm up while Robin took first base. This meant he would not start, of course; else he would be chasing Mr. Elliott's fungos and pegging to the various bases.

"Bring it in," Chase called out. The Crimson starters threw to home plate in turn and ran to the dugout, surrendering the field to the umpires.

Chase smiled down at his sweating charges.

"Remember now, we have never lost a game in these uniforms," he said. "Here is how we go. Holloway, shortstop; Mattingly, third base; Lance, pitching; Elliott, first; McNew, second; Warren, catching; Dorsey, center field; Pearson, right; Purnell, left. The base coaches will be Scott at third and Reagan at first."

The umpires returned to the field. Robin studied them curiously; this was his first game with professional arbiters. They looked stern and forbidding. No boy was apt to dispute their decisions. Then he chose a helmet and went to his coaching station.

"Leading off for Winston, Bob Holloway."

Bob was small for his age, but equaled any shortstop in the league in fielding ability. He crouched low, offering a small target, and often walked. But not today. Curt Cooley pitched carefully. The called strike brought the hit-away sign. Bob punched a grounder to shortstop Ed Burton and was out at first. Mattingly and Lance went down swinging, and Winston's first inning of the season was a row of goose eggs.

Lefty Lance walked two batters but struck out Cooley and escaped trouble by stout support from Holloway and second sacker McNew. Robin was back in the coach's box before Bruce selected his bat. Nothing-nothing. He sighed. Winston would play a lot of close games this season. The boy who had studied baseball records since his seventh birthday knew the Crimson could be compared to the championship White Sox team featuring Nellie Fox and Luis Apparicio. Winston had everything but plate power and reserve pitching. The latter was not too important unless something happened to Lefty or Bruce, or a game went into extra innings. The pair could hurl a total of only twelve innings a week.

Bruce led off with a walk. Ed McNew sacrificed and Robin nodded understanding of his stepfather's signal. Send the runner in on a single. And that hit came. Catcher Warren lifted a pop fly over second. Three Dodgers tried for it but none could reach it. Nor could any trap the ball immediately. Bruce scored easily and Steve reached second.

Another single, Robin yelled to Stu Dorsey. The word from the dugout, though, was to take no chances. Steve was the slowest runner on the team.

And Stu was one of the weakest hitters, but stayed in the starting lineup because of his fine fielding and sure throwing arm. He laid down a bunt and almost caught the Dodger infield too deep. They hadn't expected a sacrifice with one out. There was no play for Steve at third.

Chase stepped out of the dugout, asking for time. Then he gestured to Robin.

"Yes, sir?"

"Bat for Pearson. Be sure to report to the umpire."

Robin gulped, then grabbed a bat. He knew exactly what to tell the head arbiter.

"Scott hitting for Pearson."

The announcement came over the loudspeaker. Robin bit his lips and took several practice swings. His stepfather's signal was to hit away and Robin swung at the first pitch. His ground ball was in the hole between short and third. Steve scored easily—there was no play for him. Robin held first.

The announcer again: "David Reagan batting for Maury Purnell."

Bust it, Dave, whispered Robin. We are the two boys Chase picked to provide clutch hitting.

Stocky blond Dave did even better in his first Little League appearance. Dave lifted a long fly to left center. Robin was running with two out, of course, pounding hard instead of watching the ball. He gained second and there was Maury Purnell waving him on from the third base coaching box. He kept gesturing frantically. Robin turned third sharply and now he looked for the batter in the circle. Bob Holloway was gesturing him to slide. Robin hit the dirt and felt no tag. Only then did he look for the ball. The throw from center had come in wide. The pickoff player was chasing it while Dave tore on to third.

Two-nothing. Bob fluffed the chance to score another run, but the two tallies loomed big on the scoreboard.

Robin went to right and Dave to center. An inning later both were back in the dugout and Stu and Maury had returned to their original positions.

"Good work, Rob. Fine hit, Dave." Chase's voice and manner were still calm. "I knew you could give us the hits we need."

Rob ducked his head. Why couldn't Chase have left them in for at least another turn at bat? How could he be sure that two runs would be enough?

Stu Dorsey saved the lead with a spectacular catch in the third. Pearson turned a low curving line drive into the final out of the Dodgers' fourth inning. Bob Holloway and Dick Mattingly took care of the fifth frame with stellar stops and sure throws. Lefty did the rest himself. His control improved as the game went on. He was invincible in the sixth, fanning three straight batters, and the Reds' two runs stood up. Winston had broken its opening game jinx.

Chase waved his players into the dugout after shaking hands with Mac Collins. The Crimson manager sat on the steps and his gray eyes twinkled at each boy in turn.

"That's how we have to win this year, the hard way," he told them. "We must scramble for every run we get and then fight to hold the lead. Nice game, Lefty. How does it feel to start off with a shutout?"

The sweating boy blushed. "I don't feel too proud of myself, Mr. Alloway. I sure had a lot of help."

"Sure," nodded the manager. "And Bruce will get help Monday, too. As long as you two don't throw gopher balls, we'll be in there every game." He stood up. "A fast lap now and then your soda pop. You've earned it this day."

Was there a huskiness in his voice? Robin could not be sure. He joined his mother after circling the field and gulping his drink. She hugged him.

"You were wonderful, sonny boy."

He wished she would not be so affectionate before so many people. And should the pinch hitter who had driven in his team's first run be called "sonny boy"? He pulled away.

"Your hair is all messed up," he said critically. "You must have gotten excited."

"Excited!" She sighed. "I never went through such an ordeal in my life."

"I didn't think you liked baseball."

"Young man," she said severely, but with a smile, "you are learning entirely too much from your stepfather. Do you want to go home with me or with him?"

"I came on my bike," Robin explained.

"So you did. I suppose the truth is," she conceded, "I have been excited all day." She stood up. "You hurry home. I want to hear how it feels to be the star of the team."

He was hardly that, Robin thought ruefully. He had knocked across a run, sure, but Lefty was the real hero.

He had left his bicycle standing behind the left field

fence. He started toward it, only to be stopped by Mark.

"That sure was a good hit," Mark said. He hesitated. "I take it back—all I said about your stepfather letting you play."

"Forget it," Robin said gruffly. But he was more pleased than he showed. It had bothered him to be on strained terms with Mark.

"We lost," Mark said unhappily. "I didn't think we would but ——" he shrugged his shoulders.

"What happened? We didn't see much of the game."

"We had 'em to start with. Joe Pittman hit two home runs and Ramon shut them out for three innings. But Mr. Tracy wanted to go three-three. Joe was wild. They caught up with us in the fourth and went ahead in the fifth."

"Who pitched for them?"

"Joe Carlson."

"All the way? Wasn't he wild?"

"Some. We helped him."

"Did you play any?"

"One inning."

Robin kicked down his bicycle stand. "I'd better head on home. Want to come with me?"

"Sure," Mark said. A grin touched his face. "If I went straight home, I'd have to take my suit off right now."

"Me, too," Robin nodded. "We can play some catch."

CHAPTER 10

Onward Crimson Players

The Reds met the Calumets on Monday, the winner to hold undisputed first place. Robin hurried into his uniform and to the field as soon as school was out. Still he wasn't the first Winston player in the dugout. Maury, Bob and Wright were already there, wishing for a ball. Others vaulted the fence—Eddie, Steve, Stuart, then Bruce. Was he ready to throw a shutout? The stocky towhead grinned. "You'd better get some runs," he said.

"We'll catch Evans," muttered Steve. "I'd rather hit Joe Carlson anytime."

Robin knew what the catcher meant. Burly Steve was baffled by curve balls, and Wilbur was a slightly built youngster who depended mostly on roundhouses, bloopers and letups. His strong points were control and stubbornness. Most of the Crimson regulars were curveball hitters, Robin mused. His lips tightened. He wasn't. Nor Dave.

Chase and Mr. Elliott arrived together. The Red manager called his players into the dugout before starting batting practice.

"You will have to earn every run you get," he warned. "Stand up in the box, wait for the curve or letup, just poke at it."

He and Mr. Elliott threw nothing but roundhouses in batting practice. Robin hit four solidly; Dave did almost as well. Maybe, Robin mused, Chase would decide to let them start against the Calumet ace.

But no lineup change except Lefty and Bruce swapping defensive positions.

Bruce was a steadier pitcher than Lefty, though not as fast nor as versatile. Fielding held up behind him— Bob, Stuart, McNew—good glove men, gloated Robin, as were all Crimson starters. Their efforts enabled Bruce to hold Calumet scoreless through three innings. And slight Wilbur Evans let a curve hang inside on Lance; over the right field fence it sailed.

Robin sighed. No use expecting Chase to substitute before Winston got a runner on base. Then McNew walked to open the Crimson half of the third. His chance was coming, gloated Robin. Probably Reagan's, too. For Warren was signaled to bunt. It might work out just the way the first game did.

But it didn't. Evans' curve broke in too low and away from Davis's mitt. Ed took second. Warren bunted the next pitch and McNew made third with one away.

Robin looked hopefully to his stepfather. Chase appeared to hesitate, then came out of the dugout. This time Robin was ready for the manager's gesture.

"Lay it down," Chase said tersely.

The pure squeeze was impossible, of course; Ed could not lead off base. But Chase had worked out his own version. The runner on third came off with the bunt and held to see if there would be a play at first. If so, he stormed on in.

The Calumet defense knew what to expect. And Sneaker Kane signaled his infield to hold the runner at third. Robin's bunt was right to first baseman Joe Carlson. Joe played Ed back to third instead of racing for the bag.

No hit, Robin thought with regret as he stood on first. No official scorer could rule it anything but a fielder's choice.

He was not surprised to see Dave Reagan replace Maury Purnell, nor that Dave took the first pitch to let Robin advance unchallenged. Now came the same bunt play again. Dave's roller was scooped up by third sacker Hal Wilson. Apparently Sneaker Kane had changed his defensive strategy, for Hal threw to first. Or was it pure confusion? For Carlson had to scamper back to the bag and he could not spear Hal's throw. The Calumet right fielder was unprepared, too; the ball went all the way to the fence. Rob crossed the plate almost on Ed's heels while Dave took second.

Still only one out. Bob hit a hard grounder which shortstop Jim Daniel backhanded. But he made no throw, wisely, too, for Bob could travel and Dave would have beat out any throw to third.

The same bunt again. Rob chortled as the strategy worked for the third run. Dick was out easily at first.

Two away, Lefty Lance up. Hit another one, Lefty—Robin's was one of a dozen voices calling that from the dugout. But this time Hugh was offered no high pitches. He grounded to second for the retiring out.

But three big runs! They had this one in the bag, exulted Robin—but all too soon. For Ted Smith slashed a liner down the right field line. Robin got his glove on it but that was all. He did well to hold Smith at first.

He pounded his glove unhappily. Roger Pearson might have caught the ball; he covered almost as much ground as Stuart. Then Carlson exploited the other sub-stituted position. His long fly backed Dave against the fence. Dave got a hand on the ball, too, but lost control as he bumped against the wire. It might go in the books as a base hit, but Dorsey would have held the ball.

A bunt advanced both runners. Bruce struck out Barry Miller, and Robin heaved a sigh of relief. But Hal Wilson slammed a liner over second, a solid hit. Dave fielded the bouncing ball cleanly but he didn't have Stu's strong arm. Both runners scored and it was 3-2. Jim Dunlap fouled out to Mattingly and the awful fourth inning was over.

"Get on," Robin appealed to Bruce. Winston needed the runs, and Robin wanted to be sure of another time at bat.

Bruce did get on, waiting out Evans' curve, lifting a single into left. Ed promptly sacrificed and Robin stepped into the on-deck circle. Steve Warren singled through the box and Bruce beat the throw to home.

Robin looked to his stepfather. Hit away. He chuckled to himself. He could murder that curve; he was sure of it.

But he didn't get one of those breakers—instead it was one of Wilbur's few efforts at a fast ball. The pitch crossed Robin up. He lifted a fly into short center for the shortstop.

He went disgustedly back to the dugout. "Never try to outguess the pitcher, son," Chase reminded him. "He has his catcher and manager to help him; there is just one of you. And that's exactly what the odds are against you."

"Yes, sir," Rob said ruefully.

Dave flied out also and Chase reverted to his original lineup.

"We didn't do so hot today," Dave muttered to Robin. He had to agree. But they had laid down two good bunts.

And the Crimson led 5-3; that was the main thing. The stout Winston defense held that margin, too. The Reds roosted all alone on the top rung.

Atlas lost again. Jim Tracy's team at the bottom of the league standings—it was almost unbelievable. But their third game further confirmed the indications that for once the Giants were weaker than their rivals. Joe Pittman was wild again, and was hit sharply when he let up for the sake of better control. Winston gained a five-run lead without the help of pinch hitters Scott and Reagan. Atlas hitters got to Lefty for two runs in the fifth but Chase made no lineup changes. Five-two was the final score. Winston's 3-0 record dominated the league. The Dodgers beat the Cats, though, and Monday found the Crimson kids hard pressed to hold their precious position.

Robin and Dave had to get the Red attack going. That was in the fourth frame, with the Dodgers leading 1-0. Robin singled through the box to lead off the frame, Dave punched a Texas leaguer into right center. Both moved up on Bob's skillful bunt.

Robin expected the squeeze play again but Dick hit away. Successfully, too, a sharp grounder through the drawn-in Dodger infield. Dave was held at third by center fielder Gene Meador. He scored on Lance's fly to right, however, and the Reds led 2-1.

Another hectic finish, more defensive heroics by Holloway, Pearson and Dorsey. The Dodgers filled the bases in their half of the sixth but Bob snared a line drive and Stu strained against the fence to pull down Charlie Hagan's long fly.

Chase sighed as he faced his players. "That one almost got away from us," he said ruefully. "But we've had tough breaks in other games; we are due for our turn. Practice as usual Wednesday. Then what do we do on Thursday?"

"Beat Calumet!" shouted fifteen sweaty but unflinching boys.

Robin looked forward to Wednesday's practice. The drills were his only chance to challenge for an outfield starting position. His ambition was to play first base regularly, but he was reconciled to waiting another year for that. No one could blame Chase for not tampering with the combination of Bruce and Hugh. Both were solid glove men as well as dependable pitchers. But surely Chase could sacrifice some defensive strength in the outfield for sure hitting! The outfield, especially left field, offered Rob his only chance.

Dave Reagan felt the same way, of course. The team's two leading hitters in the dugout! Dave had played shortstop in the minor league but, as he conceded to Rob, there was no chance of his replacing Bob Holloway. Dave had studied baseball as closely as Robin. Defensive skill at short, second and in center field was all-important. But why not go for hitting at third base?

But Chase started the same nine players against the Cats. Joe Carlson held them scoreless, too, until Dave led off the third inning with a single, Robin went in to lay down a sacrifice and Holloway drilled one through the box. This time neither substitution hurt in the field; the Cats went down in order. And the Reds really broke out in the fourth. Lefty Lance led off with his second home run of the season. Bruce doubled and moved to third on Ed's bunt. Steve walked and Dave was up again. He flied out to left field and Bruce scored. Robin hit the ball solidly but right at shortstop Jim Daniel.

Back went Stu Dorsey and Roger Pearson to their regular positions. Some day, brooded Robin as he sat on the concrete steps, these small margins would turn out to be insufficient. And neither he nor Dave could go back in. Only starting players could re-enter the lineup.

Calumet did threaten. Reuben Potter singled to right and Jim Daniel doubled down the right field foul line. None out, runners on second and third. Robin looked anxiously to his stepfather. Would he pull the infield in or hold the boys in regular position? The latter meant conceding a score on almost any sort of ground ball. Potter was speedy; he wasn't apt to be thrown out from either deep short or second. But coming in close meant widening the base-hit area.

Manager Alloway elected to play safe, to hold down a big inning. Bruce pitched carefully to Evans but the slight Calumet star hit sharply to short. Bob made the play to second, letting a run score. Ed made no throw to first. Evans advanced unchallenged on the first offering to Carlson. Runners on second and third again. A solid hit would tie the score.

And Carlson laid into the second pitch. His line drive had base hit written all over it until Robin saw that Stu Dorsey had shifted for the batter and might possibly reach the ball. What Stu could reach, he could catch. He threw to third, holding Evans at second, allowing Daniel to cross the plate. Three-two now, still a runner in scoring position.

But Bruce had reached the weak end of Calumet's batting order. Ray Jones hit a dribbler back to the mound to end the threat.

"We need runs," Lefty Lance shouted as he came into the dugout.

They sure did, thought Robin as he took his regular coaching station. If Calumet tied the score and the game went into extra innings—with him and Dave out! He shook his head and hoped for a Winston counter-rally. None got started. And then the Cats *did* push across a run in their half of the sixth. The seventh inning found Roger Pearson on the mound, Bruce in left field. Calumet greeted Roger like a long-lost cousin. Two doubles and a single produced two quick runs. The bases were full when Holloway speared a line drive for the third out.

Manager Sneaker Kane did what Chase could not afford to do, used his second twelve-year-old pitcher in relief. Robin reconciled himself to the results. Dorsey, Pearson, Purnell—none of them could hit a curve. Stu fanned. Chase turned to his ten-year-olds in despera-tion. Sam Goldstein batted for Roger and popped out. Wright Hartung surprised Robin by singling to right. But then Bob rolled out to first unassisted and the game was over. The Crimson victory string was broken.

Chase tried to put on a cheerful front as he faced his squad.

"We can't expect to win *all* the close ones," he said. "We're still in the saddle, remember that. Laugh this one off and let's get ready for Atlas."

The manager could not follow his own advice, though.

"Don't take it so hard," his wife gently scolded at dinner. "Good heavens, you're not supposed to win every game."

"I know," he sighed. "But I thought we had this one wrapped up." He shook his head. "If we can't hold the other team, we can't win."

"One game and you act like it's the end of the world," she chided. "I never saw a first-place manager with such a long face."

"I am the first manager you ever paid any attention to," he said with a show of his usual spirit.

"And I didn't know what I was letting myself in for," she sighed.

CHAPTER **11**

A Wild Scramble

Aᴛʟᴀs ᴜᴘsᴇᴛ the Dodgers and Winston held a two-game lead again. Mr. Tracy had won with Joe Pittman, saving Alvarez for the league leaders. But Hugh Lance matched him strikeout for strikeout through two innings. Then Dave went in to bat for Dorsey and Robin crouched in the circle as a replacement for Roger.

But the clutch hitters worried Alvarez not at all. He retired Dave on a called third strike and the best Robin could manage was a dribbler to first. Robin pounded his glove as he took left field. His average was down to .333, respectable still, but by no means sensational. Dave could claim the same mark. Even so, mused Robin, they were outhitting any starter. Lefty might be hitting three hundred but no higher. How could they win a pennant with no better hitting than that?

Then he had another worry, a deep fly off the bat of

Joe Pittman. Robin pressed against the chain link fence and jumped as high as he could, but still couldn't reach the ball.

The burly Joe trotted around the bases. Robin watched him enviously. This husky blond boy was burning up the league with his bat. His team might be in last place but he led in batting, home runs and runs batted in.

Lefty walked a batter, then steadied down and retired the side. Only one run, but the way Alvarez was chunking ——

Suddenly, though, he was not pitching that way. He walked two successive batters. Second sacker Jones muffed an easy roller and the bases were jammed with Hugh Lance up. Ramon struggled to keep the ball low and outside. This he did, but in doing so he missed the strike zone. The third free pass let in the tying score. Bruce hit to shortstop Daniel who speared the ball off balance and threw wild to home. Two more Crimson runners crossed the plate to make the score 3-1, still with no outs. Ed flew out to center and it was 4-1.

Finally Alvarez regained his control. He struck out Warren and forced Paul to pop up.

But the one bad inning was enough. Lefty blanked the Giants the rest of the way.

Winston was very near to cinching the first half with three games left. Victory over the Dodgers would do it.

That apparently wasn't in the cards. Bill Roberts held the leaders to two runs and four hits, including singles by Robin and Dave. Meanwhile the usually dependable Red defense blew sky high. Even Bob Holloway and Stu Dorsey were guilty of wild throws. Five errors and as many hits produced seven Dodger runs.

Chase managed to be philosophical about this debacle.

"There had to be a day when we fell apart," he assured his players. "Let's be glad we got it out of our systems and settle down Thursday. We are still running the show."

Especially was this true after Atlas beat the Dodgers again, mainly because of two more homers by Joe Pittman. All three of the other teams now had four losses. One more Crimson victory would cinch first-half honors.

The next game brought that victory. Calumet had to pitch Evans, and his control was off. Walks to McNew and Warren in the second set up the situation Chase wanted. In went Dave to pinch hit for Dorsey. Reagan's double down the foul line scored two runs.

Robin was already on his feet, expecting to bat for Roger. That had been Chase's pattern so far, but now he changed it. Pearson stayed in the game and moved to center field after the Reds were retired.

Robin sank back down on the steps. Maybe his chance would come later.

But it didn't. Lefty kept setting down the Cats. He gave up no walks and the Crimson infield had recovered its speedy efficiency. A diving catch by Stu helped considerably.

And Bruce added an insurance run with his first

home run of the year. The final score—Winston 3, Calumet 0.

The game announcer promptly confirmed the Reds as first half winners. The final week of play mattered not at all.

"I'm glad we sewed it up today," Chase said that night. "I can ease up on Lefty and Bruce next week and give Roger some experience. And play the younger boys."

Robin bit his lip. What about trying him and Dave in starting roles?

His mother voiced his thoughts. "You can play Robin more, too, instead of just an inning at a time."

Robin started to point out that he hadn't cracked the lineup this game. Dave was a hit ahead of him now, leading the whole club in batting average.

"Sure," nodded his stepfather. "I can let him have a turn at first base. And Dave at third."

Robin suppressed his sigh. Why not in left field, where he stood a chance to play regularly?

The other managers also experimented the next week, letting all boys play, trying out new pitchers and catchers. The result was four ragged games, with plenty of scoring, errors and walks. Robin played four innings of each game at first base; Dave saw equal service at third. The two eleven-year-olds continued as the club's leading hitters, too. Robin had three for seven, Dave two for six.

The only honor at stake was second place, rather

empty laurels indeed. It went to Mac Collins' team with two victories. The Atlas Giants finished last, their poorest showing in league history.

Two days had been set aside for a possible playoff; Manager Alloway had hard practices instead.

"We are starting a new half Monday," he reminded his players. "It will be tougher going than we've had, yet we must do even better. We won this half with a 6-3 record. We can't expect to get by that easy again. And yet we can't change our game. The only thing we can do is improve it."

Robin sighed. We can't change our game! That meant nine more contests of riding the bench until a scoring opportunity was set up. His gloom must have showed finally, for his mother asked about it that night after Chase left for a directors' meeting.

"Why so unhappy, Robin?"

Robin had become bored with the television fare and had turned off the set.

He tried to evade her at first. "Oh, nothing much. Just a hard practice."

He did not deceive her for an instant. "That's odd," she mused. "Hard practices seem to bother you lately. At the start of the season you couldn't get enough baseball in any one day. Has the thrill of Little League worn off?"

Robin shook his head. "I would like to play more," he confessed.

"So would the other substitutes, honey. Look at Luther, Sam and young Jim Holloway. They have hardly showed their faces out of the dugout this year."

Robin nodded. He wanted to point out that none of these boys were strong hitters either.

"You mustn't expect too much," his mother went on. "You went to tryouts not even sure you would get on a team."

True again, Robin conceded silently. But now he had proved himself. He bit his lip. He certainly did not want to cause any more family unhappiness.

"I'm all right," he claimed. "As you say, the other boys want to play, too. I'll just have to walk my horses until next year."

"That's the attitude to take," approved his mother. "I know Chase is proud of you, both as a player and a boy. The fact is, he wants to make you legally his son."

Robin frowned. "How can that be done? He isn't my real father. How can anybody make him that?"

"It can be done—according to law, that is."

"What difference would it make?"

"None really—to you or me. Just to him."

Robin sighed. "I don't see much point in it. He is my stepfather and I don't see what going to court ——"

"Then forget it," his mother said quickly. She gestured for him to come sit beside her on the divan; in fact, she insisted upon it. Then she held him tightly. "Tell me the truth, Robin. Aren't you happier than you were a year ago?"

No reason to even hesitate about that. "Golly, yes," he said.

"That's what I wanted to know. That's what I have to

keep knowing, too." She refused to release him. "How would you feel about a little brother or sister?"

The question startled him. He looked at his mother in wonder. Was she joking? Obviously she wasn't. And why hadn't he considered this prospect before?

"I would like it," he said finally. "Especially a little half brother."

Her lips curved in a smile. "It might just happen that way. But little sisters can be wonderful, too, dear. My older brother was crazy about me. I wasn't over four years old when he took me fishing. I remember my mother was worried to death."

The words brought recollections to Robin, too, of his own father. The Scott family had been happy fishermen—not sports fishing so much as leisurely experiences along creekbanks and the Colorado River. His mother had insisted that she could catch as many fish with her cane pole and worms as could his father with casting rod and box of artificial lures. Robin remembered her teasing challenge: "I don't need all that fancy equipment. I just cut a cane pole, tie on my hook and catch fish."

"If it's a little half sister," he promised, "I'll take her fishing. Your big brother must have taught you plenty; you could pull them in."

"He did. He taught me just like Chase taught you baseball. He showed me no quarter because I was a little girl or because I was his sister, either."

Robin sighed. He knew what had happened to that uncle. His mother never failed on Memorial Day to visit a grave in Oakwood Cemetery. And she still treasured a worn newspaper clipping which briefly described how Lieutenant Edward Conway had been shot down over the English Channel.

"You had to grow up all alone, didn't you?"

"Yes," she said quietly. "And then—your father. I had reconciled myself to never knowing any other happiness except being your mother. Then Chase came along. And now——"

Robin suddenly returned her embrace. "We are doing fine," he declared. "We are doing—just fine."

And so they were, he reassured himself as he went upstairs to bed. It was wonderful to have his mother always smiling again, not finding her sometimes staring off into empty space, her lower lip tight, a far-off look in her eyes. He would help keep her this way, too; she would never hear another word from him about his substitute's role. But going to court—whatever that meant—no point in that. They were doing all right this way. He didn't go to sleep immediately. Nobody could say that he hadn't earned his uniform, nor that he got any concessions because his stepfather managed the team. He drew a ripple of applause from Winston supporters every time he entered a game as a pinch hitter. So did Dave. The league's official scorer had compiled and distributed full records of first half play. He and Dave had been responsible for a full third of Winston's scores. It was not exaggerating at all to claim that two pinch hitters had batted the Crimson to a first half title. That thought was enough to fall asleep on.

CHAPTER 12

The Giants Rise Up

THE REDS started the second half as they had the first, by eking out a close decision over the Dodgers.

But there was one difference, a small one to most people perhaps, but to Robin a very important item. Chase seemed to have settled on Dave as his first substitution, reversing his early strategy. Reagan delivered, too, driving in the tie-breaking run in the fifth. Robin had been told to get ready; Chase called him back to the dugout after Bruce scored to give Winston a 3-2 lead. Robin struggled to hide his disappointment and was sure that he did.

Lefty Lance set down the Dodgers one-two-three in the top of the sixth. The Crimson was off to another good beginning.

But Tuesday, sitting with several of his teammates, Robin realized that the second half would not be a duplication of the first nine games. The difference would be in the Atlas Giants. Mr. Tracy's team walloped the Calumet Cats 8-1. Loose play did not account for the wide margin, either; the Giants hit for their scores, with husky Pittman clouting a bases-full home run.

Robin rode home with his stepfather, who had reached the field in time to watch the final four innings. He wasn't surprised by the Giant showing, said Chase. He had expected all along that Atlas would be the team to beat.

"They can play for the big inning," he said. "Pittman, Cannon, Davis—three big boys in a row, any of them apt to knock the ball out of the park. If Joe settles down as a pitcher ——"

He shook his head. "I sure don't want any one-game playoff with them for the title. When Alvarez has a good day, they are tough, very tough." He sighed. "We have our pitching problems, too."

Robin knew what his stepfather was thinking. Roger Pearson had been hit hard in his every mound appearance. Winston had bench strength in hitting and fielding, but not on the mound. And both Lefty and Bruce had shortcomings. Hugh was apt to be wild in the early innings and Elliott lacked the big pitch, the stuff to blaze by a batter for the third strike. And with the team's only three-hundred hitters in the dugout—Robin's lips tightened. He must not start brooding about that again, especially not at home.

Calumet might be easy for the Giants to beat, but the

Cats stiffened against Winston. Chase had predicted it, of course; all teams would be "laying" for the Crimson this half. Calumet had saved Wilbur Evans for the Reds. His tricky curves deceived the Winston starters as usual.

But Bruce pitched steadily in his turn. He gave up a single run in three innings, and that might have been avoided except for one of Bob Holloway's rare errors.

Thus far the Crimson had gotten only two players on base, and those after two out. But Lefty hit one against the right field boards to open the fourth. Quick recovery by fielder Jim Dunlap held Lance at second.

Bruce bunted—the sacrifice was nearly automatic for this Crimson team. Ed McNew stepped into the box confidently; he was not dismayed by breaking stuff. He slammed a double into left center and Lefty scored standing up. Steve hit a rather weak roller to shortstop Daniel, who elected to try for the lead runner. There was no force and Ed slid in safely.

Chase stood and gestured to first base. Robin bit his lips. So Dave was first choice again! Why? And if Reagan scored both runners, then there would be no point in a second pinch hitter. Robin would sit out another full game.

Dave took the first pitch to let Steve move to second. Evans tried two low outside pitches and missed with both. Two-one. Dave stepped out of the box and wiped his hands. Robin tensed as Evans toed the rubber. This was the pitch for Dave to hit. Odds were it would be over; the Cat ace was usually stingy with his walks.

It *was* over, a slow-breaking curve. Dave cracked it, too. But this line drive streaked squarely into the waiting glove of second sacker Ray Jones. Two out now.

Roger Pearson was in the on-deck circle. Robin saw the right fielder turn to the dugout instead of going toward the plate. Then Chase got time out and motioned to his stepson.

Robin lingered over his bat choice. Chase would want him hitting away, of course. And he had flopped in his last pinch batting role against Wilbur. He had used a 33-inch bat, expecting a curve, and had been caught napping by a fast pitch.

Still he wanted a heavier bat than usual. The Cat defense would be shifted for him to pull. And, regardless of what Evans threw, he would not have the speed of Joe Carlson, Bill Roberts or any other regular league starter.

Robin finally settled for a thirty-two. He reported to the umpire and carefully set himself forward in the box. The Calumet defense was pulled around as he had expected, the third baseman close to the bag, the left fielder almost on the foul line.

If he could hit a bit late—he held back his swing even though the pitch was right over. There he went again, trying to outguess the pitcher. He rubbed his hands in the dirt, stepped back into the box. He would worry about meeting the ball squarely and nothing else.

Evans, a strike to the good, tried his usual bait, a pitch breaking low and outside. Robin refused to bite.

The Calumet hurler went to the resin bag. Robin stepped out of the box. This slender Calumet boy used almost every device in the pitching repertory, including taunting deliberateness. He took his time getting back on the rubber, too. Robin forced himself to patient waiting. Finally Wilbur toed the rubber.

He tried to deceive Robin with the same ruse which had succeeded before. He fired his version of a fast ball right over the plate.

It didn't work this time. Robin met it solidly. His line drive was squarely over second base. Straight-away center was open, too, because of the overshifted Calumet defense. The ball went all the way to the fence. Two runs scored. Robin was sure he could have reached second, but the first base coach held him up.

Then Maury Purnell struck out to end the rally. Chase gestured for Robin to take left field and Maury to move to center.

Three-one. Lefty Lance, mused Robin, would be almost a cinch to pitch them in from here. But Bruce did not get stronger as the game wore on. Especially did his curve ball seem to lose its effectiveness in the later innings.

And Calumet's power was up—Daniel, Evans himself, husky Ted Smith.

Chase gestured to Robin to play deep and swing toward center. The other two Crimson outfielders were straight-away, which meant that Bruce would be throwing fast balls almost exclusively. The left field line was open if the batter could pull.

And Jim Daniel did just that. Robin started quick; some instinct had him moving before he heard the crack of the bat, certainly before he had the line drive gauged. It was a back-handed play for him, too, a diving sort of catch unless he chose to stop and let the ball drop in for a single.

Chase had drilled his outfielders to go all out on such plays, Robin did just that. He grabbed for the ball knee high and could not hold his footing. Down he tumbled, but he gripped the horsehide tightly.

Applause came from the stands, approval from his Crimson teammates. Robin slowly went back to his regular position. He nursed a grin and shot a look toward the Crimson dugout. It surely had not weakened the Winston defense this time for him to replace a starter! Maybe, after that catch, Chase would let him stay in for the rest of the game.

But not so. When Bruce finally weathered the inning —he allowed a single and walked a batter—the Crimson manager returned both Stu and Roger to the lineup.

It made sense; Robin conceded that. Calumet's weak hitters were up; Bruce was working on a two-run lead. But how could Robin perform any better than he had? What must a boy do to stay in the game for Chase Alloway!

Robin was hopeful that the Dodgers could beat Atlas, especially since Ramon Alvarez had already pitched his allotted six innings for the week. But Joe Pittman was a different pitcher this half; somehow

Manager Tracy had succeeded in polishing all weaknesses. And that Giant power! Joe hit a home run, as usual; he was challenging the league record with his consistent circuit clouting. The Dodgers could have overcome this blast, however. The home runs hit by Will Davis and Tony Cruz spelled the difference. Tony's drive was particularly damaging. Manager Collins had ordered Ramon passed purposely with Will already perched on second and two away. Tony's first homer of the year accounted for three runs and brought the score to 6-2.

Robin was sitting between Roger and Eddie.

"I wanted the Dodgers to win," said Roger, "but I'm glad for Tony's sake. I know how it feels to have the hitter ahead of you put on base so they can pitch to you. I'll bet nobody does that to Tony again."

That was how the game ended—6-2. Two unbeaten clubs would clash Monday. And who could deny that this improved Giant team must rate as slight favorites even over the first half winners? Maybe, Robin reflected, Chase might decide that Atlas had to be outscored and make more use of his and Dave's potent bats.

But Manager Alloway held firm to a respected baseball policy, never change a winning game. He started his same nine players against Atlas and kept them in all the way. Eddie's third inning homer scored Bruce ahead of him and those two runs were enough. Hugh Lance handcuffed the Atlas power until the last of the sixth, when the amazing Pittman hit another homer, this time on a pitch which actually fooled him. Lefty threw in his change-up and caught the Giant slugger off balance. He recovered enough to swipe at the pitch, and still had the power to propel the ball over the fence.

Chase shook his head. "Even when you fool him," he groaned to his assistant manager, "he can hit it out of the park. What do you do about it? You can't walk him all the time."

"We can be thankful there is just one of him," said Mr. Elliott.

One gone, and only a one-run lead! Robin was concerned, but not distressed. Hugh was still pitching strong, and he was past Pittman. But Paul Cannon and Will Davis were emerging as sluggers, too. The Reds were not home by any means.

Paul blasted a liner to left center; Maury Purnell took it against the wire. Will connected solidly, too, but a running catch by Roger turned his drive into the third and final out. The Crimson was still winning all the close ones.

"Practice again Saturday," Chase told his squad. "We're a game to the good but we can't let down. If we do, we'll be tied with Atlas and we can't afford that. Look what they almost did to us today. Two runs don't mean a thing against their power. A foot more and Paul Cannon would have had a home run himself."

Maybe the Giant pitching would falter and either the Dodgers or the Cats would upset them. But even as Robin voiced that hope to his stepfather, he did not expect it.

"That sure would help," agreed Chase. "But we'd better not count on it. We'd better depend on our own efforts. If Joe Pittman keeps improving on the mound——"

And he did. Pittman blanked Calumet the next Monday, allowing only two scratch singles, walking only three batters. Meanwhile his mates took over slugging responsibilities; Joe couldn't as the Cats walked him in all three trips to the plate. The 7-2 decision left no doubt as to the second half picture. It would be Atlas and Winston right down to the wire.

Robin overheard Mr. Thomas talking to Mr. Fenton, the league's official scorer.

"This won't make sense if the Reds hold their lead," said the president. "Atlas will dominate the all-star team. I can think of five Giants who deserve places, while Lefty Lance is about Winston's only standout."

"It's one year when statistics don't mean a thing," agreed Mr. Fenton. "I brought all the averages up to date last night. The Reds don't have an individual leader in anything, nobody close to it."

But they still had the best team, Robin said to himself. They topped this second half with a 3-0 record compared to the Giants' 3-1. As for the all-star team, Mr. Thomas might be right. Lefty played fine first base in addition to his pitching. His batting mark of .270 didn't show up too well when compared to the other averages, but Lefty had delivered in the clutches. Bruce might rate consideration as a fielder but what about his .250 record at the plate? Bob Holloway and Stu Dorsey were the league's best in the field, but Bob was hitting only .200, while Stu was usually the first starter pulled for a pinch hitter.

The Reds were indeed an unusual league-leading team, agreed Rob. Its only two dependable hitters played only an inning of any game, might not even get into the lineup at all.

CHAPTER 13

The Showdown Is Set Up

Bruce Elliott met the challenge of the Bedford Dodgers, holding a good-hitting team scoreless for three innings, allowing a single run in the fourth. That tied the score, for Hugh had poled another home run in the first frame.

Had any other league team ever played so many close, low-scoring games? Robin doubted it. He had never read of a championship march on 2-1, 3-2, and 4-3 victories. Perhaps it had been that way in the era of the so-called dead ball, when ten or twelve home runs in a season meant recognition as a super-slugger. But not in recent times, surely.

Bob Holloway led off the fourth with a scratch single. Dick Mattingly started to the plate, but was called back. To bat, instead, went Dave Reagan.

Robin sang out encouragement, and sincerely. But, at

the same time, he wondered again why Dave was his stepfather's first choice for a pinch hitter. Their batting averages were identical, with Robin holding an edge in bunting dependability. And surely that was the Winston strategy now, to advance the runner.

It was, but Dave muffed the assignment. His poke was right to pitcher Bill Roberts, giving the hurler time to make the play at second. One away.

Lefty singled to center and Dave was held to a one-base advance. Both runners moved up on a passed ball. Bruce laid down a trickler. Pitcher Roberts fielded it off balance, hesitated, then made the play at first. Dave tore for home and slid in to gain the umpire's decision. Bunting, good base running, expert sliding—boy, reflected Robin, they had worked those fundamentals overtime.

Bill Roberts lost his control suddenly; his first pitch to Eddie hit the dirt and eluded Dick Flanagan. Hugh came sliding in for run number three. Then Eddie slammed Roberts' next offering over the left field fence. Golly, gloated Robin as he shook Eddie's hand when the grinning boy reached third, they were breaking all their own records this game. Four runs already, including two circuit clouts!

Manager Collins came out of the dugout and in came Curt Cooley to take over mound duties. Robin sighed. Calumet and Bedford were going all out to make things tough for the Crimson. Talk about ganging up on the leading team! Both Dodger twelve-year-olds were being used in an effort to check Winston.

It was a futile effort, however, for Bruce continued his careful pitching and the Crimson defense held firm as usual. Cooley had no trouble with Winston hitters, either; he squelched the fourth inning outburst and kept out of trouble himself.

But the damage was already done. Final score: Winston 4, Bedford, 1.

Nursing a three-run lead, Manager Alloway had not risked another substitution. He had returned Mattingly to the lineup as soon as the rules allowed and the nine starters finished the contest. Robin Scott, now the team's leading hitter, had sat out another full game. Dave's average had dropped slightly because of his failure to advance the runners.

But Robin was careful not to show his disappointment. At the next game he led the Crimson contingent which sat in the stands and silently prayed for a Dodger upset of the awesome Giants. Chase cautioned them against any vocal display; never, he said, did he want his players rooting in the stands. But he could not prevent their wishing; in fact, he watched hopefully himself.

But the Giants could not be wished out of contention. Joe Pittman turned in another stout pitching performance. The 7-2 victory left the Reds a half-game in the lead, and still two more games to play with the Giants.

Chase had to call on his bench to start a winning rally against Calumet. Dave was his first choice again; this time he cracked a single which scored Ed from second base. Robin got the bunt sign; he advanced Dave with a trickler to third. Maury Purnell blooped a Texas leaguer into right, moving Dave to third. Bob Holloway punched one over second to make it two runs.

The two-run lead lasted only an inning, however. Lefty walked Reuben Potter with one out. Shortstop Jim Daniel met Hugh's first offering for a fence-clearing blast. A pass to Ted Smith brought Chase out of the dugout.

"I hope he doesn't pull Lefty," whispered Dave, sitting on the steps beside Robin.

Robin nodded. Lance even on an off day was a better pitcher than Roger.

That was Chase's decision, too. And Hugh pitched his own way out of the crisis. Whatever his manager had said to him got results. Hugh fanned two batters and was tough in the first half of the sixth. But Winston went scoreless, too; it was 2-2 as the Reds came in for their half of the inning.

Lefty led off, and Robin joined in the clamor for the southpaw to win his own game. He almost did, too; his line drive thudded into the chain link fence in right center. Lefty, running hard and sliding, gained second.

None away, clean-up hitter coming to the plate. The usual strategy would be to let Bruce hit away, but he wasn't that dependable at the plate, no matter what his place in the batting order. Robin was not surprised to get the sacrifice signal from his stepfather.

Bruce pushed the ball toward first. He was an easy out but Hugh got to third unchallenged.

Chase came out of the dugout and motioned to Robin. The boy was a bit startled; he had not replaced Eddie before. Would Chase signal him to bunt again? That was it. Lay it down, hope the Cat defense would allow Lefty to score. Or, if not, put another Crimson runner on base. Robin nodded and took a deep breath. He would like to hit away; a fly or a hard grounder would score the winning run and the Calumet infield was in tight. But signals were signals. He dumped the ball a few feet in front of the plate.

Lefty had come off third with the bunt, crouched waiting to see if catcher Smith threw to first. The Cat receiver thought he could catch Lefty off the bag. He threw hard to third, but high and wide. Hal Wilson deflected the ball and Hugh tore in for the decisive tally.

Had he been credited with a base hit or a fielder's choice? Robin listened for the game totals to find out. He doubted himself that Ted could have thrown him out at first.

But apparently Mr. Fenton thought otherwise. No hit, but no time at bat either.

"Nice work, boys," Chase told them. "That's our game—keep the pressure on them and hope they blow. We'll practice Saturday as usual. And next Tuesday ——"

They knew what he meant. Tuesday's pairings sent

them against the Giants. And victory would mean a two-game bulge with three contests left.

But slight, swarthy Ramon Alvarez took over Tuesday's proceedings. He struck out the first three Crimson batters as a starter. He had a no-hitter into the fourth, when Chase sent up his pinch batting aces. Dave ahead of Robin, of course; the latter was accustomed to that now, though still not reconciled.

Dave's sharp grounder was plucked off by shortstop Pittman for the first out. Robin reported to the umpire and set his feet deep in the box; Ramon could fire the ball even if he weighed less than a hundred pounds.

A foul back against the wire, a dribbler wide of third base for strike two.

Then Ramon broke over the best curve Robin had seen in the entire season. He had fallen away from the pitch, sure that it would be a ball. But the umpire gestured that the curve had caught the inside corner and the batter was out.

Maury Purnell rolled out to Alvarez and the Giants were within six outs of victory. For Lefty had yielded two runs in the first inning. He had retired Mark and Pete Stahl, then had walked the menacing Pittman, not purposely, but making sure not to offer him anything good. The caution with Joe proved Hugh's undoing. For Paul Cannon, though hitting late, poled one over the right field fence.

Two-nothing. The Reds were getting a dose of their own medicine, Robin thought ruefully. The Atlas defense was solid behind Ramon's consistent chunking.

Dick Mattingly spoiled the no-hitter with a sharp single in the hole between short and third. But that was the extent of the Winston offense. Chase left Dave and Robin in to bat a second time but the Crimson bench flopped this day. And the Giants had added an insurance run in their half of the fifth.

Three-nothing. The Giants now shared first place in the second half standings!

Chase managed a grin for his disappointed youngsters. "We can't win all the close ones," he said gently. "You tried, and this wasn't our day. Practice Wednesday as usual. This is still our show."

Was it? Not from where Robin watched the Giants hammer out a 6-2 win over Calumet the next Thursday. It was an easy victory for Joe Pittman, who also homered to come closer to the league record.

But the usually impotent bats of the Crimson regulars came alive Friday. Hugh had a double and a single, Bruce a home run, Eddie a two-bagger, two infield hits for Holloway. These, coupled with hard base running, added up to five runs. Meanwhile Bruce pitched steadily and the Red defense was tight as usual. Dick Flanagan's circuit clout was the Dodgers' only tally.

Bruce had to go again the following Tuesday, against the Cats, for Lefty must be saved for the showdown with the Giants. Another steady performance, two scratch runs by the Crimson starters, and the 2-0 decision kept the Reds even with Atlas, who had pounded two Dodger hurlers the previous day for a 9-4 decision.

Identical records for the Giants and the Reds— seven victories against one defeat! The Crimson had improved its first half record, reflected Robin, but even that might not be enough. Friday's game would tell the story. Atlas had Alvarez ready; Chase could counter with his ace lefthander.

Robin and Dave drank their soda pops together after the game. "I wish we could have played," Dave said. "We haven't had any real batting experience in a week."

They had taken their regular turns in practice, but not against opposing pitching.

Robin choked back any reply.

"I hope we win Friday and get this business settled," his mother said that night. "It's beginning to get me down."

Chase had gone out to meet a client, and Robin, already in his pajamas, was watching television. The boy nodded glumly. He wanted the season over, too. Then let the all-star team be chosen, probably with no more than one or two Crimson players on it. Chase would manage it, of course—if Winston held off Atlas. Then he would have solid hitters in his starting lineup—Joe Pittman, for sure, Paul Cannon, Dick Flanagan, Charlie Hagan. He would have a team that could hit away for its scores instead of having to squeeze out a run at a time.

"I know how you feel," his mother said. "I wasn't supposed to get emotionally involved with the team. But I can't help it." Her eyes searched his face. "I wish you could be happier about the baseball season."

"I'm happy," Robin claimed.

"You're putting up a good front," she conceded, "but you don't fool your mother."

He decided to say nothing.

"It has been quite a strain on Chase, too," she commented. "I suppose the only way to learn about Little League managers is to marry one—and to have your son on his team. Then you're dealing with two sets of problems." A twinkle came into her eyes. "Especially with a team like this one," she went on. "See how much I've learned about baseball? As Chase said, a mother becomes an expert right away."

He really didn't want to discuss the team, nor even think about it. Probably he would not even play tomorrow; certainly he wouldn't start. And if a pinch hitting situation came, Chase would call on Dave first.

"Every game," she sighed, "has been such a close one, this half especially. Chase has had no opportunity to let his substitutes play."

Again Robin said nothing, but his lips tightened. If her remarks were meant to soothe him, they failed. It certainly never hurt Winston to "let" him play. Who had batted in more runs? Who had delivered better in clutch situations?

"You have been a strong asset to the team," his mother went on. "Chase appreciates it. Believe that, honey."

"I know he does," Robin said lightly. "I'm just like you. I just want us to win tomorrow and stop the strain."

CHAPTER 14

Winner Takes All

Robin squirmed in the dugout, wishing there was something he could do. The Crimson regulars were hustling through their infield, their voices forming a steady chorus. Around the horn—try for two—cut off at home! Four infielders reacted quickly to each command from the tall man slashing out the grounders. Mr. Elliott was as busy, hitting to five boys in the outfield. Robin sighed. This meant that Chase intended to use Dave Reagan and Wright Hartung as first substitutes.

Robin decided to straighten the bats, just to be doing something. The hurt was still there despite his mother's reassurances. Did he really deserve no more than this, to be idle in the dugout along with the younger boys while Winston got ready for this crucial game? He sighted his mother but turned his head quickly. He was afraid his disappointment showed in his expression and attitude. She must not realize that her words of the previous night had had little effect.

That strong Crimson bench! It may have helped during most of the season, but Chase hadn't made a substitution in the last two games. Never tamper with a winning combination! It made sense, sure. But it did not ease the heartache of a boy who ached to play and thought he should be playing, going in for an inning at least.

Bring it in! Winston's warmup time was gone. Lefty came to the dugout, pulling on his Crimson windbreaker. The two umpires came through the third base gate. Mark Kelly and Pete Stahl emerged from the Atlas dugout and started swinging bats. The announcer called out the starting lineups.

Robin could not help trembling. A Crimson victory would wrap all this up. Winners of both halves—what a reward for Chase Alloway, who had taken so many lickings so graciously! Sentiment generally favored him; Robin had heard support for the Reds voiced many times during the past two days. But those same voices reminded Chase that Jim Tracy's teams always finished strong. This one surely had, brooded Robin. The Giants had been easy to beat the first half, finishing last. But the Blue team had caught fire. Robin sighed as he recalled the last Atlas-Winston game and the shutout pitching of Ramon Alvarez.

"Everybody down."

Chase's voice seemed calm, but Robin sensed the

manager's tenseness. His eyes swept the row of young faces.

"What do you say, boys? Let's pick up all the marbles and go home."

With that he waved his starters onto the field. They leaped out of the dugout with loud "yippees." Solid applause came from the left stands and some handclapping from the opposite section. They like Chase in this league, Robin thought proudly. They should.

Lefty finished his warmups, rubbed his fingers on the resin bag, faced the first batter. Get the first one in there, Lefty! If you get behind on the batter and have to ease up—Robin shivered. Substitutes had butterflies in their stomachs, too.

"Strike one!"

Mark had been taking. He cut at the next offering. Lefty easily fielded the slow roller and tossed to Bruce.

Keep going, Lefty! Robin shouted it hoarsely. The lithe pitcher fanned Pete Stahl, got two strikes on Joe Pittman. They were going down one-two-three, gloated Robin. Then he groaned in despair. For Joe connected solidly and there was no doubt where the ball would land—in the cedar clumps beyond the left field fence. Around the bases trotted Joe; out poured his Blue teammates to greet him at home plate. From the loudspeakers came Mr. Thomas's voice:

"Ladies and gentlemen, Joe Pittman has just set a new West Austin Little League record for home runs in a single season!"

Chase stood up and gestured for his six substitutes to

do the same. Robin's lips trembled. The Winston bench rising to applaud an opposing player! How many other managers would make such a gesture?

Paul Cannon struck out and Lefty came to the dugout, disgust written all over his face.

"I was trying to pitch him low," he explained to Chase. "But it was letter high and ——"

He shook his head and slumped down on the steps.

"One run won't beat us," Dick Mattingly vowed. "You've got it today, Lefty boy."

Robin echoed the same confidence, but as he went to the third base coaching box he could not feel as sure as he sounded. One run *had* beaten them in their last meeting with the Giants. And Ramon Alvarez started out as strong as in that other game. Bob, Dick and Lefty marched to the plate in succession and Lefty did foul off two pitches. But none of the trio hit a fair ball. Three batsmen, three strikeouts!

Robin went slowly back to the dugout. Chase forced a weak smile.

"You didn't get any business, did you?"

"No, sir."

"Ramon is snapping that curve," the manager pointed out. "Start throwing with Dave, Rob. I may have to put him in."

Put Dave in! Robin choked back his sob. But his "Yes, sir," came out firmly.

He could guess what his stepfather was thinking. If a Crimson runner got on base next inning, Stu Dorsey would be in the cleanup spot. And Stu couldn't hit a curve for sour apples. Dave was apt to hit Ramon's kind of pitching. Robin tried to suppress his scowl. He had done well against curveball pitchers, too.

Lefty walked Will Davis. Alvarez, a good-hitting pitcher, slashed a grounder through the box. A clean hit—so it seemed. But Bob Holloway dived and managed to trap the ball. He could never have gotten the runner at first, but, with another desperate lunge, he touched second with his hand. The lead runner was out.

Robin could only shake his head in admiration. Chase's "glove boys" were hard to beat, even if they were hitless wonders. The beaming Lefty struck out Tony Cruz, but Bret Murphy hit a solid smash toward dead center. The runner was going with two out, of course. Robin's heart was in his mouth as Stu Dorsey raced backward. Stu strained against the fence, then leaped and stretched. He toppled downward and for an awful second Robin feared a bad injury. But Stu scrambled up quickly, gesturing to the umpire with his right hand, holding up his glove for the arbiter to see. The ball gleamed white against the worn leather. The base umpire hesitated as if unwilling to believe his own eyes. Then he gestured the batter out, and the applause for slender Stu came from both sections of the bleachers. What if he couldn't hit a lick, gloated Robin. Stu had cut off two certain runs, for he had speared the ball as it zoomed over the four-foot barrier. Lefty waited to hug the center fielder and run in with him.

Get on somehow, get something started! Come

around to see me, Robin yelled to Bruce Elliott. Bruce took a ball, then a strike. The third pitch broke in; Bruce dragged it between first and second. The play was close, but the umpire's hands stretched out flat in the safe signal.

As Eddie McNew came to bat, Robin caught the signal from his stepfather. Bunt, of course—what else when his crack fielders didn't hit their weight? Eddie laid down a perfect sacrifice. Another gesture came to the third base coach. If the batter hits one by the infield, send the runner on in. But Steve Warren missed three straight pitches, and there were two out.

Robin guessed the reason for the delay in the Winston dugout. He looked away, and down. Dave Reagan was coming in to pinch hit. Robin shut his eyes tight. Why Dave instead of him?

He blinked away his tears to meet his responsibility as coach. The same strategy was still in force. Bruce nodded as he stood with one foot on second. He wouldn't even look at the ball, but at the base coach.

Strike one, a foul back against the screen. Dave had an eye for a curve, conceded Robin. He would get wood on the ball, some kind of wood. Ball one. Dave didn't fish at a low drop. Alvarez poised, delivered ——

Crack!

The ball streaked past the Atlas shortstop. Robin waved and danced and Bruce never turned to look or slow up. Around third—this boy could move. The outfield peg came in hard and true, but the coach who had spent so much time teaching his boys how to slide was rewarded. Catcher Davis lunged to tag the runner but Bruce had feinted, then slid in from the opposite side. Safe! The tying run went up on the board. The grim Alvarez fanned Roger Pearson to retire the side, but now the victory was up for grabs again.

Chase's next substitution was announced before Robin reached the dugout.

"Now playing center field for the Reds, Wright Hartung."

A ten-year-old! Certainly he could cover ground, but hadn't one Robin Scott showed up well in outfield practice, too?

"Good coaching, Rob," Chase called out as the boy came toward the dugout.

Robin slumped down on the bench after congratulating both Dave and Roger. They made room for him between them.

"I hope Wright doesn't bobble one," muttered Roger. "He's fine for a ten-year-old, but ——"

"I wish you had gone to center," Dave told Robin. "You're more dependable than any ten-year-old."

"No, sir," Roger said firmly. "Mr. Alloway knows what he's doing. I can go back in next inning. If Robin were in now, he couldn't go back into the lineup. We wouldn't have his bat as an ace in the hole."

Robin's eyes widened. At the moment he hardly dared believe that explanation.

Roger talked on. "We've done the fielding, sure. But who's knocked in our runs in the close ones? Reagan and Scott, that's who. We all know it."

"I haven't played in three games," Robin pointed out. "I've just been to bat four times this whole second half."

"Your dad hasn't needed you," shrugged the left fielder. "But just get your hitting britches on. Your dad makes sense. He plays it by the book."

Robin trembled as he realized that Roger's analysis was absolutely true. Except that Chase was his step-father, not his ———

Then he leaped up with the others—in both dugouts. Bob Hester's line drive streaked over second. Wright could reach the ball, all right, but only with a back-handed stab.

All sank back to their seats as the ten-year-old substitute performed like a professional, making the difficult catch look easy. Lefty Lance then struck out Mark and forced Pete to hit an easy dribbler to second base. Lefty was getting stronger, gloated Robin as he pulled on his helmet and ran to his coaching station. The southpaw ace usually did. The early innings gave him the most trouble.

But Ramon was the same type of pitcher. Purnell, Holloway and Mattingly went down in order.

The announcer's voice again: "Returning to center field for the Reds, Stuart Dorsey."

More applause for the fielder who caught balls already over the fence.

Joe Pittman was up next for Atlas. Robin groaned. Out went Chase for a quick word with Lefty. The pitcher nodded and carefully followed instructions—no intentional walk but keep the ball low and outside. Lefty's effort at 3-1 was low and Joe trotted to first.

Paul Cannon advanced the runner with a fine bunt. Lefty called for time, used the resin bag, then poised, his features grim. And just as grimly he pitched to Will Davis—three straight strikes, and there were two away. Then it was up to pitcher Alvarez. His hard drive would have been caught by very few Little League center fielders, but slender Stu Dorsey made it look like just another ordinary catch.

Our strength is up, chortled Robin. Just one run, one measly run, and then six outs and ——

Lefty Lance almost put his team ahead single-handed, but his drive lacked a foot of clearing the fence. However, the Crimson pitcher reached second standing up and Robin was almost beside himself. Any sort of hit—he strained to catch his stepfather's signal. Chase wanted the runner to play safe. It made sense, mused Robin. Lefty was no speedster. The sacrifice was a smarter call.

Strike one! Bruce couldn't even bunt a good curve. The batter squared around again but stepped back quickly. The pitch was into the dirt and Will could not trap it. Lefty reached third without even sliding.

Robin looked again to the bench for instructions. But, instead of giving a signal, Chase was asking for time out. Then he was gesturing for Robin to come in. He hesitated a moment. Why? He knew every signal and could be trusted ——

The game announcer understood Chase's purpose before Robin did.

"Pinch hitting for the Reds, Robin Scott!"

A ripple of comment swept the crowd. Robin could guess why. Pulling his cleanup batter for a pinch hitter—what kind of strategy was that? Then some recalled that Robin was a sure bunter, Jim Tracy among them. Out came the Giant manager to confer with his pitcher and infield.

Chase put his arm around Robin. "They will expect you to bunt. They will play in tighter than usual. Start to square around, but hit the ball if it's in there. Don't go for a wild pitch."

He slapped Robin's shoulder. "If I'm guessing wrong, it's my fault, not yours. But if I'm right, and you meet that ball squarely ——"

Robin nodded, his lips trembling slightly. He decided to use a 33-inch bat and choke up. His stepfather wanted a hard grounder or a short liner, not a home run.

The Blue infield came in as Chase had predicted, came close in. Alvarez followed probable orders, too; he threw high and wide. Robin swung around as if to bunt, then pulled back. Ball two!

Robin stepped out of the box and rubbed his hands in the dirt. Ramon would not try to make him fish again. This pitch would come in with all Alvarez had.

And it did. The ball broke sharply. Robin feinted his swing around, then straightened up and poked at the horsehide. It was a good poke. The Giant second baseman could have reached it from his normal position, but Tony Cruz was in on the grass. So was first sacker Pete Stahl. Lefty Lance cavorted home while Robin stopped at first base.

He called for time and pretended to retie his shoe laces. But that was not his real motive. If this was the winning run—and it might well be—who deserved the credit, all the credit? Robin blinked and bit his lips. It would be all Chase's doing, and not just because of his successful strategy. He took a poor sort of stepson, Robin reflected, and made him not only a ball player but other things as well. And half the time, anyhow, I have failed to appreciate him!

He signaled that his shoes were tied and play resumed. Ramon Alvarez bore down even harder. Three straight strikeouts ended the inning.

"Playing first base for the Reds, Robin Scott!"

Of course, Robin thought, pulling his mind back to the game. He had to man the position for a full inning. Bruce brought him the first baseman's mitt.

With the score 2-1, Lefty Lance showed no mercy to the weak end of the Blue batting order. Three up, three down.

In the Red half of the fifth Alvarez walked Pearson, but Purnell's bunt effort turned into a pop-up for a double play. Then Bob Holloway struck out.

Back in the dugout as the fateful sixth began, Robin watched his stepfather's every move. They had only three outs to go. Come on, Lefty! The southpaw had his work cut out for him, Kelly, Stahl and Pittman in that order. But give Hugh Lance a one-run lead and three batters to retire—he was really a pitcher then. Mark fanned. Pete lifted an easy fly to second. Then it was Joe Pittman, the strong boy, the record holder. Robin shut his eyes. Why did it have to be Pittman?

He would get nothing good, that was certain. Lefty was aiming for the low outside corner and made no bones about it. A called strike. A ball. Ball two. Then Joe swung at a low breaking pitch, trying to golf it. It rose high and Robin's heart stopped beating for an instant. It was deep, too, very deep. But Stu Dorsey was against the fence, ready to leap up if necessary. Then Robin saw the center fielder take a forward step and dared to breathe again. If Stu was coming forward ——

The catch, the umpire's wave, a melee of red-capped boys in the infield, a sad-faced group of youngsters bravely offering congratulations, then trooping toward their dugout one by one. And proud parents crowding onto the field, overwhelming Chase with their plaudits. The first, of course, was blond Janet Alloway, who had declared she would never get involved in baseball.

"Into the dugout, boys," Chase called out. "Everybody back, please."

One boy could not obey, not immediately. Janet Alloway held her son as tightly as she did her husband.

Mr. Thomas was already at home plate with the huge championship trophy. Robin finally squirmed free of his mother and joined his teammates in the dugout.

"Golly," gloated Lefty, "look at that cup."

Mr. Thomas held up his hand for silence. "Will the

manager of the champions come to the plate, please?"

Robin looked and there was Chase still accepting congratulations, acting as if he had not heard. Robin leaped out of the dugout and tugged at the manager's arm.

"Dad, Mr. Thomas wants you at home plate."

"I know."

Robin did not notice the look which passed between Chase and Janet Alloway.

"Go on, Dad," Robin urged. "Go get that cup for us. We can gab later."

"All right, son," Chase agreed. He called out to his players. "Line up, you knuckleheads!"

But his wife still did not release his arm.

"Did you hear him?" she whispered. "He called you Dad twice."

"I heard him," Chase said gently.

She squeezed his arm again. "You've already gotten the big trophy. Now go out and get that gaudy bauble and we'll see how it looks on the mantel."